Members Only

JULIUS DROPPED TO ETHAN'S FRONT STEP, panting. "Let's face it," he said to Ethan cheerfully. "When it comes to sports, you and I are losers."

Ethan laughed, because Julius had a way of making everything he said sound funny. But Ethan hadn't missed every single basket. He had gotten at least half of them— well, some of them. He might not be as good a basketball player as Peter, but he wasn't as bad as Julius, either.

"We could form a club," Julius went on. "It would be open only to losers. Like, you'd have to be bad at a certain number of things to qualify. You'd have to miss the most baskets in P.E., and read the shortest books for English class, and have the worst experiment at the science fair."

"We'll call it . . ." Julius broke off, as if waiting for a brilliant idea.

"Losers, Inc.," Ethan suggested.

"That's it!" Julius said. "I'll be the president, and you can be the vice president. Unless you want to be president?"

"Nah. The club was your idea." Besides, Ethan figured, it was more loser-ish to be vice president than president, even of a club for losers.

Losers, Inc.

Losers, Inc.

Claudia Mills

SCHOLASTIC INC.

New York Toronto London Auckland Sydney
Mexico City New Delhi Hong Kong

ISBN 0-439-11024-6

Published by Scholastic Inc., 555 Broadway, New York, NY 10012, by arrangement with Hyperion Books for Children, an imprint of Buena Vista Books, Inc.
SCHOLASTIC and associated logos are trademarks and/or registered trademarks of Scholastic Inc.

12 11 10 9 8 7 6 5 4 3 2   9/9 0 1 2 3 4/0

Printed in the U.S.A.   40

First Scholastic printing, September 1999

To Jonathan Reingold

Losers, Inc.

One

Ethan Winfield straightened his shoulders as he stood against the measuring tape on the back of the kitchen door, trying to make himself taller. He placed his hand on top of his head, glad for once of the blond cowlick that refused to lie flat. Then he turned around and checked where his fingers had touched the tape. Four feet, ten and a half inches.

Still four feet, ten and a half inches. He hadn't even grown a quarter of an inch since his mother had made the most recent mark on the chart back on his twelfth birthday, two months before, in November.

Ethan let his eyes fall on the tape again. His brother, Peter, was only two years older than he was, but at fourteen, Peter was a full eight inches taller. "Of course Peter's taller. He's two years older!" Ethan's mother had told him the last time she heard him complaining about his height. But when Peter was twelve, he'd been two inches taller than Ethan was now. Also, Peter had always had better grades and a shelf full of sports trophies. It wasn't fair.

This past year Ethan had begun writing a book called *Life Isn't Fair: A Proof*. It wasn't a real book, just a list of experiences that made Ethan and his best friend, Julius, wonder whether the universe had something in particular against the two of them. For example:

Monday, January 20. Julius Zimmerman didn't have his math homework to turn in. Mr. Grotient said, "I'll have to take five points off for that, Zimmerman." Lizzie Archer, AKA the Lizard, didn't have her math homework to turn in. Mr. Grotient said, "Well, turn it in first thing tomorrow, Lizzie."

Tuesday, January 21. Ethan Winfield made six perfect baskets in a row on the playground before school. During gym class, when Coach Stevens was watching, he missed six baskets in a row.

Wednesday, January 22. The cafeteria ran out of dessert. The last person to get a dessert was the person right in front of Ethan Winfield and Julius Zimmerman.

Thursday, January 23. Ms. Leeds called on people in alphabetical order to give their book reports, and everybody got theirs over with except for

Ethan Winfield and Julius Zimmerman, who had to go all by themselves the next day.

Friday, January 24. When Ethan and Julius finally did their book reports, Ms. Leeds told them that the books they read were too short, even though she never told the class ahead of time that the book-report books had to be a certain length. Ethan's book had 64 pages. Julius's book had 72 pages. The Lizard's book had 276 pages.

The notebook was almost full. Usually Ethan had at least one unfair thing to add to it every day. Now he could add that he hadn't grown even a quarter of an inch in two whole months. Maybe he had stopped growing. Maybe four feet ten and a half inches was going to be his full adult height, and he would spend the rest of his life shorter than every single sixth-grade girl, except for the Lizard, who apparently hadn't grown since she starred in *Thumbelina* in second grade.

Ethan poured himself a bowl of cereal and drowned it in milk. He had read that some farmers were giving their cows a special growth hormone that showed up in the milk. He took an extra swig from the jug before putting it back in the refrigerator, just in case.

It was a tradition in the Winfield family that Ethan and Peter made dinner every Saturday night. The tradition had begun when they were both still in elementary school. Back then Saturday night dinner had usually been frozen pizza, topped with whatever the boys could find in the refrigerator. But lately the dinners had been real food, prepared from real recipes in real cookbooks.

When Ethan came downstairs after a long, boring hour spent struggling with math homework, he found Peter in the kitchen, flipping through *The Joy of Cooking*.

"How about Swedish meatballs?" Peter asked. "Over noodles. And there's some stuff in the fridge for a salad."

"Sounds good," Ethan said. He was hungry already. But Peter was always the one who decided what they would make. Ethan peered down at the open page of the cookbook. "Or how about Hawaiian meatballs? Over rice."

Peter shook his head. "We don't have any pineapple."

"Did you look? Sometimes Mom stores extra cans up high."

But when Ethan searched the pantry shelves, he didn't find any canned pineapple. Canned pears, canned peaches, canned fruit cocktail. No canned pineapple. He should have known better than to bother checking. Peter was always right. It was one of the most annoying things about Peter.

As Ethan began mincing the onions for the Swedish meatballs, he tried to remember if Peter had always been right, even way back when they were little. All of Ethan's memories were the same. Peter racing ahead on his two-wheel bike, without any training wheels, as Ethan struggled behind on his small plastic tricycle. Peter swimming the length of the big pool as Ethan clung to his inflated tube in the baby pool. Not that Peter wasn't nice. He was nice. Almost too nice sometimes. But many of the entries in *Life Isn't Fair: A Proof* mentioned Peter.

Ethan had made two just that morning:

Saturday, January 25. The regular West Creek newspaper, not the dumb *West Creek Middle School News*, had a picture of Peter Winfield on the front page of the sports section, scoring in Friday night's basketball game. Ethan Winfield has never even had his picture in the dumb *West Creek Middle School News*.

Saturday, January 25. One girl from Peter Winfield's class called him seven times on the telephone. No girl has ever called Ethan Winfield. Of course, Ethan Winfield does not want any girl to call him. Ethan Winfield would hang up if any girl called him. But it is still true that no girl has ever called him.

As it turned out, the Swedish meatballs were delicious. Ethan had three helpings, spooned over hot, buttery noodles. Ethan's dad had three helpings, too.

"You boys could open a restaurant," Ethan's mother said. "If you ever want a job cooking for Little Wonders, let me know." Little Wonders was the preschool where she worked as a teacher. "Our kitchen staff could definitely use some new ideas. What else did you two do this afternoon?"

"Nothing," Ethan said.

"Nothing," Peter said.

It was one of their favorite replies to their mother's questions.

"Peter, I saw you got a letter from Representative Bellon in the mail. Was that anything interesting? Had you written to him about something?" she asked next.

Ethan almost never got any mail. But last year he had written to Representative Bellon about gun control, for a fifth-grade assignment on writing the business letter and the friendly letter. Representative Bellon had written back, thanking him for his concern. Ethan still had the letter.

"Actually," Peter said, obviously trying not to look too pleased, "he was congratulating me on placing third in the state on that math thing I did last fall."

"Oh, honey! Go get the letter. We want to see it!"

Peter rolled his eyes at Ethan, but he retrieved the letter from his room and handed it to his mother. She read the letter out loud, then passed it to Ethan's father. Ethan's father didn't say anything, but he beamed at Peter.

"We have to frame this!" Ethan's mother said. "We can hang it in the hall, with all of your school pictures." Then she stopped and looked quickly at Ethan. "Do you still have *your* letter from Congressman Bellon?" she asked him. "We can frame both of them."

"No," Ethan lied. "I threw it away."

He was going to throw it away, too, as soon as he got to his room. His letter was nothing like Peter's. Everyone in his entire class had written a letter to Congressman Bellon, and everyone had gotten the same letter back. "Dear _____. Thank you for your concern about _____. Caring young citizens like you are vital to the future of America. Sincerely, Andrew Bellon." The only kid who had gotten a different letter had been Lizzie Archer. Somehow even Representative Bellon had known that you couldn't write back to the Lizard with a form letter.

His mother gave Ethan a worried look. He pretended not to see it. He carried his empty plate to the dishwasher. Then he slipped upstairs to make another entry in his book.

On Sunday afternoon Julius came over to shoot baskets at the hoop on Ethan's garage door. Although it was January, the bright Colorado sun sent the temperature soaring into the sixties, melting the snow that had fallen the day before.

Ethan made a few baskets, but he missed plenty, too. Julius missed every time. Unlike Ethan, Julius was tall for his age, but his long arms were spindly and awkward. When Ethan watched Julius play basketball, it began to seem physically impossible that any human being could actually catch that large round ball and throw it anywhere near, let alone through, a hoop that was hung so high and hard to reach.

Finally Julius dropped to Ethan's front step, panting. "Let's face it," he said to Ethan cheerfully. "When it comes to sports, you and I are losers."

Ethan laughed, because Julius had a way of making everything he said sound funny. But *Ethan* hadn't missed every single basket. *He* had gotten at least half of them—well, some of them. He might not be as good a basketball player as Peter, but he wasn't as bad as Julius, either.

"We could form a club," Julius went on. "It would be open only to losers. Like, you'd have to be bad at a certain number of things to qualify. You'd have to miss the most baskets in P.E., and read the shortest books for English class, and have the worst experiment at the science fair."

Ethan laughed again. He and Julius always *did* read the shortest books for English class, and they always *did* have the worst experiment at the science fair. He had to admit that the club sounded perfect for the two of them. "And math," he added. "You'd have to get the most problems wrong on every math test."

"We'll call it . . ." Julius broke off, as if waiting for a brilliant idea.

"Losers, Inc.," Ethan suggested.

"That's it!" Julius said. "I'll be the president, and you can be the vice president. Unless you want to be president?"

"Nah. The club was your idea." Besides, Ethan figured, it was more loser-ish to be vice president than president, even of a club for losers.

"We need a motto, too," Julius said. "Like 'Winning isn't everything.' Or 'Losers, and proud of it.' "

Ethan had a sudden inspiration. "I have it: 'Some are born losers. Some achieve losing. Some have losing thrust upon them.' "

"Did you make that up?" Julius demanded suspiciously.

"I heard it somewhere," Ethan said. "About greatness. You know, some are born great . . ."

Peter rode his bike into the driveway, home from a hike in the mountains. "Hey, Ethan, Julius," he said. "How's it going?"

"Okay," Ethan answered for both of them.

Still on his bike, Peter held up his hands for the basketball. Ethan threw it to him. From halfway down the driveway, Peter took aim. The ball arched gracefully through the air and swished through the net without touching the backboard.

So Peter was perfect. What else was new? Ethan was glad that he and Julius had formed their crazy club. There was something satisfying about being a founding officer of the one organization of which his brother could never be a member.

Two

On Monday morning, Ethan biked to school behind Peter and met Julius by the bike racks. Sometimes Ethan and Julius shot baskets together before school; today they just sat on the curb at the edge of the blacktop. Ethan scuffed his feet in the dirty sand dumped there after Saturday's snow.

"Hey," Julius said in a low voice. "Look."

Ethan looked up. He didn't see anything. Peter and his eighth-grade friends were shooting baskets at the far hoop. A bunch of girls watched them, giggling together. Farther along the curb, Lizzie Archer was sitting all alone, her wild red curls hanging down over her face. She was scribbling something in the notebook that she always carried with her. Probably she was writing a poem. The Lizard was always writing poems.

"Over there," Julius said.

Then Ethan saw her. She was tall, around Peter's

height. Maybe twenty. Or even older. Old enough to be a teacher. But she didn't look like any teacher Ethan had ever seen. The most unteacherly thing about her was her hair. It fell down her back in long, shining, silky waves, almost to her knees. She looked like Rapunzel. And her hair was pure gold, as if Rumpelstiltskin had spent all night spinning it out of straw. Her face was beautiful, too. And her clothes were beautiful. On top she wore a big, bulky sweater, but under it she wore a thin, swirly, shimmery skirt, even longer than her hair. She stood watching the kids at play.

"I think"—Julius spoke in a thick, trancelike voice— "I think I'm in love."

This was not the first time that Julius had been in love. Julius had already been in love with two movie stars, one lead singer in an all-girl rock band, and a checkout cashier named Stephanie who worked at King Soopers. Ethan couldn't take any of Julius's love interests very seriously, but at least none of them had lasted more than a week or two. Rapunzel was definitely the best-looking one yet.

The bell rang. Ethan and Julius joined the crowd of sixth graders. Ethan saw Rapunzel enter the school by the front door.

In homeroom, during morning announcements, Ethan found himself wondering what someone like Rapunzel was doing in West Creek Middle School. She was too young to be somebody's mother. Maybe she was somebody's sister. Or a substitute? Ethan had never seen a substitute with hair like that.

On the way to first-period science class, Ethan and Julius looked into every classroom off the main hall, hoping for another glimpse of Rapunzel. They didn't see her. But when they turned into the science room, there she was, deep in conversation with Mr. O'Keefe.

"Good morning, class," Mr. O'Keefe said when all the students were in their seats. "I'd like to introduce our new student teacher, Ms. Grace Gunderson. Ms. Gunderson will be working with you for the next five weeks, as part of her teacher training at the university. She's going to explain what she has planned for us."

"Good morning," Ms. Gunderson said. Her voice was as beautiful as her hair, and face, and skirt. It was soft and low and a bit husky. Ethan glanced over at Julius. Julius looked ready to faint.

"I'm going to be working with you on your science fair projects," Ms. Gunderson went on. "I think you all know that the West Creek Middle School science fair will take place on Thursday, February 27. I hope some of you develop projects that will be chosen for the regional science fair or even the state science fair. But most of all, I hope this will be a chance for all of you to learn more about the beauty and wonder of science."

If Mr. O'Keefe had ever talked about the beauty and

wonder of science, Ethan would have snickered. He wasn't snickering now.

Ms. Gunderson explained more about how the science fair projects should be organized. Then she said, "Now I want you to form small groups for brainstorming about science fair ideas. I'll be circulating among your groups to begin talking with each of you individually."

After they had counted off, Ethan found himself in the first group, with three other boys—not Julius—and two girls, including Lizzie Archer. Ms. Gunderson pulled her chair over to join them.

"In science we start out with questions," Ms. Gunderson said in her low, throaty voice. "What questions about our physical world would any of you like to try to answer?"

Ethan had plenty of questions, but he kept them to himself. Why wasn't he growing? How come some people were better at things than other people? How could anybody have hair that long and smooth and silky without a single tangle?

No one else said anything, either, even the Lizard, who usually talked all the time in class with great, embarrassing gusts of enthusiasm. But she was more enthusiastic about English and social studies and art than she was about science.

Finally David Barnett spoke. "Well, I guess—maybe something about electricity. Like dry cells. Or batteries, or something."

"Do you have a particular question you would like to ask about electricity?" Ms. Gunderson asked.

"Not really. I just like to hook up wires and stuff."

"Electricity, then!" Ms. Gunderson gave David an encouraging smile, but Ethan could tell that, five minutes into her first day as a student teacher, she was already feeling discouraged.

"Anybody else? Remember, today we are just brainstorming. You don't have to have a well-formulated hypothesis you plan to be testing. We're just looking for a question, a *real* question, something you would really like to find out."

Lizzie raised her hand. "I'd like to know whether—well, this really isn't a science question, exactly—but whether . . . You see, I write poetry sometimes . . ."

All the time, Ethan thought.

"And there's this strange thing that happens when I write it. It's like I hear this voice in my head, telling me the lines to write down, and I write them down just the way the voice says. So I'm wondering where that voice comes from. I mean, where do the words *come* from when I write a poem? Sometimes I think I must have heard them somewhere else, and I'm just remembering them. I get afraid sometimes that I might be copying somebody else's poem, you know, without meaning to. Sometimes I even look in books to try to find the poem, but I never can, so I must be making it up. But it doesn't *feel* as if I'm making it up. It feels just like I said, like a voice talking to me in my head."

"So your question is . . ."

"Where the voice comes from."

"That's a very interesting question," Ms. Gunderson said slowly. She sounded a bit bewildered. People often became bewildered when they were around Lizzie. "Some people might not think of this as a scientific question, but I think a true scientist is someone who is interested in *all* questions about the physical world. Do any of you have any idea how she might proceed?"

"She could go see Mr. Jonas," Alex Ryan said snidely.

Everybody laughed, except for Ms. Gunderson and Lizzie.

"Mr. Jonas?"

"He's the school shrink," Alex explained with a mean smirk. "People who hear voices in their heads should see a shrink."

The others laughed again, but this time Ethan didn't. He didn't want to laugh at anything Rapunzel didn't laugh at. And Lizzie looked ready to cry.

"Lizzie could write to other poets," Ethan heard himself saying. "She could try to find out if they have the same experience. She could, you know, kind of do a survey or something."

"That's a wonderful idea . . ." Ms. Gunderson paused for his name.

"Ethan."

"That is a wonderful idea, Ethan." When she said it, Ethan felt that she meant it, that he was the kind of person who had wonderful ideas all the time. The way Ms. Gunderson was smiling at him, Ethan felt smart and brave and strong and kind, as if he could climb to the top of the highest tower with no ladder other than her hair.

If this was what love felt like, he was in love.

Ethan floated through science class and art. Then, in third-period math class, he came down to earth with a thud.

Mr. Grotient was a short, roly-poly man who always wore a bow tie and suspenders. He looked a little bit like an inflatable toy, held down by beanbag weights stuffed into his small, shiny black shoes.

"Boys and girls," he began, rocking slightly on his toes, "today we are going to begin a new program called Peer-Assisted Learning."

Ethan looked over at Julius. He could tell that Julius didn't know what Peer-Assisted Learning was, either.

"In Peer-Assisted Learning, students work together in pairs as Peer Partners. Peer Partners study together during class several times each week."

Ethan met Julius's eyes again. They never worried about having to choose partners. They always chose each other.

"I worked out your Peer Partner assignments over

the weekend," Mr. Grotient went on. Ethan began to feel uneasy. He didn't want Mr. Grotient picking his Peer Partner. He wanted to be Peer Partners with Julius.

Mr. Grotient picked up a paper from his desk and began to read. "Your Peer Partner assignments are: Lizzie Archer, Ethan Winfield. David Barnett, Julius Zimmerman. Susan Butler, Marcia Faitak . . ."

Ethan sat stunned. His Peer Partner was the Lizard. The teacher's pet. The poet who heard voices in her head. Thumbelina.

Ethan made himself look over at Lizzie. Lizzie's face was red. Was she as mad at being stuck with him as he was at being stuck with her? But she didn't really seem mad. She almost seemed to be blushing. Now that he thought of it, Lizzie had been giving him strange looks all morning, ever since he had stood up for her against Alex in science class.

"All right, class," Mr. Grotient said. "We'll use the rest of the period to get started on Peer-Assisted Learning, PAL, for short. Move your desk next to your Peer Partner's desk, and begin working together on the problems for chapter seven."

The others began shoving their desks around. Ethan watched numbly as Julius and David pushed their desks together. At that moment, Ethan was more of a loser than Julius: Julius hadn't been assigned the Lizard as his Peer Partner.

Marcia Faitak, who usually sat next to Lizzie, pulled her desk over to Ethan's side of the room.

"Ethan." Marcia said his name in a conspiratorial whisper. She waved a sheet of lined notebook paper in Ethan's face. "I found this on the floor last period by Lizzie's desk."

Marcia handed the paper to Ethan. He didn't want to read it, but Marcia plainly wasn't going to budge until he did.

He glanced down at the page and saw four lines of what had to be a poem. With Marcia's eyes boring into him, Ethan began to read:

For Ethan, My Hero

Alas, the winter wind doth blow,
But yet my love doth brightly bloom.
However cold the driving snow,
I shall love thee till my doom.

Marcia snatched the paper away. "She's coming!"

Marcia returned to her seat just as Lizzie, still blushing, pushed her desk next to Ethan's, so that their two chairs were almost touching.

Ethan didn't need to make any more entries in *Life Isn't Fair: A Proof.* He had all the proof he needed. Nothing like this had ever happened to Peter, or ever could.

It could happen only to the vice president of Losers, Inc.

He was in love with Grace Gunderson, AKA Rapunzel.

And Lizzie Archer, AKA the Lizard, was in love with him.

Three

Ethan stared down at his desk, unwilling to look at Lizzie. He knew that Lizzie was staring at her desk, too, unwilling to look at him. One of them had to break the silence. But Ethan felt as if he had lost the power of speech.

"Ethan, Lizzie," Mr. Grotient called over to them, "start working."

Ethan opened his book to the problem set at the end of chapter seven. Next to him, Lizzie opened her book, too. He read the first problem silently.

"So . . ." His voice came out in a squeak. "So what do you think the answer is?"

"Well, if y is 22 and z is 34, then x would be y over z, or 22 over 34, or you could reduce it to 11 over 17."

Ethan wrote it on his paper. At least the Lizard was good at math. He was relieved that she wasn't talking about poetry, or voices inside her head, or loving people till her doom.

"What about problem two?" he asked then.

Lizzie told him the answer in her usual rapid-fire way.

"You're talking too fast," Ethan said.

Lizzie repeated her answer, more slowly.

It seemed ridiculous to go on this way, but Ethan didn't know what else to do. "What do you get for problem three?"

"I did the first two," Lizzie said. "*You* do problem three. Besides, we're not supposed to just *do* the problems. We're supposed to talk about them."

Ethan's heart sank another notch downward. He didn't want to have conversations about math problems with anyone, let alone with the Lizard.

"What's the answer to problem three?" Lizzie asked.

Ethan took a wild guess. "Twenty-five?"

"Twenty-*five*? How did you get 25?"

Ethan shrugged. He had just made it up. "Well, if y is 17—wait a minute—which one is y?"

Lizzie began to explain the problem to him. "See?" she said when she was done. "The answer is 7. I still don't know how you could have gotten 25."

Ethan wrote down 7. Then his eyes wandered to the window. "It's starting to snow," he said before he could catch himself. He had actually said a sentence to the Lizard that he didn't have to say.

Lizzie looked toward the window, too. "Ohhh!" she breathed, as if she had never seen snow before. "The flakes look like feathers. But everyone always compares them to feathers. Maybe thistledown? Or wisps of cotton? But everyone always compares snow to cotton, too. *Wisps* is a good word, though. 'Wisps of cotton, floating down.' "

Lizzie scribbled the line right on her math paper.

" 'Falling gently o'er the town.' " She turned to Ethan. "*O'er* is a poetic way of saying *over*."

Ethan squirmed. "Maybe we should get on to problem four?" he asked. With all his heart, he wished that third period were o'er.

At lunch, Julius could talk of nothing but Grace Gunderson.

"Rapunzel, Rapunzel, let down your hair!" he moaned piteously. "I thought I was in love those other times, but they were nothing compared with this."

Ethan didn't want to talk about Ms. Gunderson with Julius. He wished Julius hadn't seen her first. He wished Julius hadn't said that he was in love with her first.

"What do you want to do after school?" Ethan asked, to change the subject.

"Nothing," Julius said in the same lovesick voice that was beginning to get on Ethan's nerves.

"We have to do *something*," Ethan said.

"I guess we could mess around with our science fair project," Julius said. "For some reason, I'm suddenly interested in anything to do with science."

Ethan noticed that Julius had said "our science fair *project*," not "our science fair *projects*." Julius was naturally counting on doing his project with Ethan, since he and Ethan always did their projects together, except when Mr. Grotient came up with some horrible surprise of his own. Why do twice as much work when you could do half as much work, and do it with your best friend, too? But for the first time ever, Ethan didn't want to do a project with Julius. Not the science fair project.

Everything Ethan and Julius worked on together turned out to be a disaster. Ethan didn't want his science fair project for Ms. Gunderson to be a disaster. He wanted it to be something that would make her look at him again the way she had looked at him in class that morning. It was probably useless to dream of doing a project that would win the West Creek science fair and be chosen for the regional science fair, but there was no law against dreaming. Something about Ms. Gunderson made him want to dream.

"Um—what kind of project do you have in mind?" Ethan asked. He didn't know how to tell Julius that he didn't want to work together this time.

"Something easy," Julius said. "And something that involves food."

"Like what?"

"Like, we could take turns blindfolding each other

and doing taste tests on different brands of potato chips or ice cream. Like, we could see if low-fat potato chips tasted any different from regular potato chips. Or if ice milk tasted any different from ice cream."

"That doesn't sound very scientific," Ethan said.

"Sure it does. Besides, when Ms. Gunderson was in our group, she said that any real question about the physical world was a scientific question."

She had said the same thing to Ethan's group, regarding Lizzie's question. Ethan didn't like the idea of Ms. Gunderson repeating herself to anybody else's group.

"Look," Julius went on, "it's not like we're going to win, anyway. We want a project worthy of Losers, Inc. And one we can eat. Right, Veep?"

"Right, Prez," Ethan said. He forced himself to return Julius's grin. But he couldn't help noticing that Losers, Inc., wasn't even twenty-four hours old, and already one of its two officers was trying to figure out how to break a rule.

After lunch, Ethan and Julius sat together in study hall, in the West Creek Middle School library. But they didn't study. Only the Lizard studied in study hall.

Julius drew pictures of Grace Gunderson in his notebook. They made her look like a long-haired Barbie doll, Ethan thought. He doodled pictures of basketball players in his own notebook. But he felt too restless to draw. Maybe he ought to pretend to be doing some library research, so he could have an excuse to get up and walk around. "Hey," he whispered to Julius. "Let's pick out the books for our next book reports, okay?"

Julius put down his pen. "Ms. Leeds said they had to be at least one hundred pages. I'm going to find one that's exactly a hundred pages."

Actually, Ms. Leeds had said more than that. Ethan still remembered the scathing tone of voice in which she had remarked, after their last book reports, "I have to say that it is *very* disturbing to find *sixth*-grade students still choosing books on a *third*-grade reading level." The words had stung. Ethan didn't read on a third-grade level. He just happened to like short books. But Ms. Leeds had implied that he was some kind of slow learner.

Ethan and Julius walked over to the fiction shelves. Julius started with the A's, taking down every skinny book and turning to the end to check the number on the last page.

"Ninety-five. Too short. One hundred fifteen. Too long. One hundred five. Getting warmer. One hundred nine. Colder. Okay, here it is. *A Boy and a Dog.* One hundred pages."

Ethan walked up and down the shelves, half looking at the titles, half looking at nothing.

"Here's another one," Julius called over to him in a

loud whisper. "*A Horse of Her Own*. Exactly one hundred pages. Do you want it?"

Ethan shook his head. "It looks like a girl's book."

"It looks like a *short* book. Okay, here's another one. One hundred three pages. There's a dog on the cover, too."

Ethan felt a strange idea forming in his brain. "It might be kind of funny, one time, to read a really *long* book." He silenced the thought that now he was suggesting breaking a second Losers, Inc., rule.

Julius stared at him.

"It would just be a joke," Ethan said quickly.

"You mean you wouldn't really read it?"

"No, I'd *read* it, but it's like, Ms. Leeds said our other books were too short, so I'd be showing her. 'You want a long book? Okay, here's a long book.' How long was the Lizard's book last time?"

"I don't know. Two hundred something."

"Well, I'll find a book with *three* hundred pages. Or four hundred. I'll be showing Ms. Leeds *and* the Lizard, too. Lizzie won't be able to stand it that I read a longer book than she did."

Ethan was standing next to the D's. "Here's one. Charles Dickens. *A Tale of Two Cities*. Four hundred twenty-two pages."

Julius put the dog book back on the shelf. Ethan wondered if Julius would tell him that he couldn't be vice president of Losers, Inc., if he read *A Tale of Two*

Cities for his next book report. But Julius didn't say anything.

Back at their table, Ethan opened *A Tale of Two Cities* to see how bad it was going to be. "It was the best of times, it was the worst of times," read the opening line. Charles Dickens could have been talking about Ethan's own life.

By the end of the day, Ethan had made three new entries for *Life Isn't Fair: A Proof.* In a black-bordered box on its own special page, he wrote:

Monday, January 27. Ethan Winfield was assigned the Lizard as his partner in Peer-Assisted Learning.

From gym class he had:

Monday, January 27. Ethan Winfield missed more baskets than anyone in the class except Julius Zimmerman. Coach Stevens said, "Sometimes I find it hard to believe that you and Peter Winfield are really brothers."

As soon as Coach Stevens had said it, Ethan could tell that the coach felt sorry for letting the words slip out. "Just kidding, Winfield," the coach said. "Come on now, concentrate! Just concentrate on the ball!"

This was not the first incredibly stupid thing that a grownup had said, comparing Ethan to Peter. One of these days Ethan was going to get a T-shirt printed that said, "Yes, I am Peter Winfield's brother. No, I am not like him in any way."

From English class, Ethan had:

> **Monday, January 27.** Marcia Faitak came up to Ethan Winfield and said, "Lizzie wrote poems about you all through social studies. Did you know that your name rhymes with *heathen*?"

After school, Ethan and Julius rode their bikes through the snow to Julius's house. Ethan ate one large bowl of chocolate ice cream and then dished himself out another. It had been a two-bowl kind of day.

"Our hypothesis could be that fat-free ice cream tastes the same as regular ice cream," Julius said. "Or that it tastes different. Which do you think it is?"

"I think it tastes different," Ethan said.

"We should probably test other people, too," Julius went on. "In case our tastes are strange or something. We could test Peter and your folks and my folks and some of the guys at school. That'd run up our ice cream bill a bit, but our parents'd probably pay if it's for school. If it's for the sake of science."

"Listen," Ethan said. If he was going to have a chance at doing a special, award-winning science fair project for Ms. Gunderson, he had to speak up now. "I was thinking—"

"Don't think!" Julius said.

"No, honestly, I was thinking that maybe—I mean, the ice cream idea sounds like a lot of fun, but . . ."

"You want to do it on something else?"

Ethan nodded miserably. He wanted to do it *on* something else. He wanted to do it *with* someone else. He didn't want to be a loser this time—like Julius. The thought was so disloyal that he felt terrible for even thinking it.

"That's okay," Julius said. "It doesn't have to be ice cream. It could be potato chips—or anything. I made up that idea in two minutes. I don't care what we do. What do *you* want to do?"

"I don't know. But . . ." *Just say it.* "We could still help each other with our projects. We could still help each other a *lot*. But maybe this time—it might be a good idea, just this once, to do our own projects."

There. He had said it. Maybe Julius would understand. Maybe Julius wouldn't stare at him with a hurt look in his eyes.

Ethan made himself look at Julius. Julius was staring at him with a hurt look in his eyes.

"Like I said, we could still help each other with our projects. Like, I'll still eat all the ice cream you want." Ethan tried to make it sound like a joke, but Julius didn't laugh.

"Sure," Julius said. "We can do our own projects. Whatever you want."

"Just this once," Ethan said lamely.

"It's okay. I understand," Julius said in a tone that made Ethan wonder whether Julius didn't understand, or whether Julius understood too well.

Four

"How was school today?" Ethan's mother asked that night at dinner.

"Fine," Peter said.

"Fine," Ethan said.

"Did anything interesting happen to either of you?"

"No," Peter said.

"No," Ethan said. But he felt a little sorry for his mother, making doomed efforts every night to generate some family dinner conversation. Family dinners were important to her—real dinners where everyone ate the same thing, instead of foraging in the fridge for snacks. And where people talked to each other instead of gobbling their food in silence.

"We got a student teacher in science," Ethan said.

His mother gave him a grateful smile. "What's he—she?—like?" His father looked up from his plate.

Ethan's dad wasn't much of a talker, but he was always a good listener.

"It's a she. She's nice."

"Long hair?" Peter asked. Ethan nodded. "I saw her in O'Keefe's room. Is Zimmerman in love with her yet?" Julius's crushes had become a family joke.

"Uh-huh." Ethan felt his own cheeks flushing and hoped no one else noticed.

"What about you, Peter?" his mother asked. "Did you tell your math teacher about your letter from Representative Bellon?"

"No," Peter said. He ate another forkful of casserole. Then he relented, too. "The game this Friday? Coach Stevens invited Coach McIntosh from the high school to see us play."

"You mean to see *you* play," his mother said, refilling Peter's milk glass from the pitcher on the table.

"Well, he didn't say that. But I think—I know he hopes I'll do a good job."

"Of course you will!"

"Just do your best," his father said. "That's all anyone can ever ask of you."

"I got a new child in my class," Ethan's mother said then. Since she was the only member of the family who liked to talk, most of the Winfield dinner conversations centered on the activities of three-year-olds at the Little Wonders preschool. Ethan couldn't remember his father ever telling a story from his carpet-cleaning business.

"Edison," she went on. "That's his name. Edison Blue. *Very* negative. His mother couldn't get him to come inside this afternoon when she was dropping him off. 'You'll be all cold and wet,' she told him. 'I *want* to be all cold and wet,' he said. When she finally carried him in, kicking and screaming, he ran right back outside again and stood in the exact same spot where he had been standing before."

"What did you do?" Ethan's dad asked. "I'd have been tempted to leave him there."

"Well, I finally got his mother to go. You can't do anything with them when their mothers are there. And then he came in after a while, when he saw that I wasn't overly impressed by his little tantrum. But I can tell that Edison Blue is going to be an interesting addition to Little Wonders. Do you boys have much homework to do?"

"Not tonight," Peter said. "I thought I'd get started on the science fair."

"Me too," Ethan said. He hoped he wasn't blushing again. Quickly he began clearing the table, just in case.

Upstairs in his room, Ethan tried to think of a project for the science fair, but he didn't know how to begin. In elementary school, he and Julius had just done whatever project their dads suggested, from a library book Ethan's mother checked out every year on award-winning science fair ideas. One year they had done something with magnets. Another year they had let mold grow on different foods: apples, bread, yogurt. That had been Ethan's favorite project. He forgot what their hypothesis had been, but he still remembered how gross the food had looked when the project was displayed in the elementary-school gym.

This year he wanted to do something different—not an experiment out of a book but one he thought up all by himself. He wanted the judges to be astonished that a twelve-year-old boy could have thought up such a project and carried it out all alone, single-handedly pushing back the frontiers of science. He wanted to be the youngest person ever to win a Nobel Prize. And when he did win, he'd say in his acceptance speech, "Everything I am today I owe to my sixth-grade student teacher, Ms. Grace Gunderson." And she would shake back her golden hair and smile at him the way she had in class today.

So Ethan knew that he wanted his project to win the Nobel Prize. The problem was, he still didn't have the faintest idea what the project should be.

As he biked to school the next day, Ethan wondered if Julius would still be mad at him. Not that Julius had acted particularly mad after the conversation about the science fair. They had watched dumb cartoons together, as they usually did. They hadn't talked much; they usually didn't talk much. But this time the silence had felt different.

Julius was on the playground first. Ethan made himself go up to him.

"Hey, Veep," Julius said, punching his shoulder.

"Hey, Prez," Ethan said, punching him back. It was good to know that Losers, Inc., was still going strong. Or as strong as it could be with its vice president breaking its rules.

"I saw her drive into the parking lot," Julius said then, lowering his voice to the lovesick sigh he used whenever he talked about Ms. Gunderson. "That's her silver Honda Accord over there. See it? Next to the red Jeep Cherokee."

Ethan glanced over at it dutifully. He was in love with her, too, maybe even more in love than Julius was, but he didn't feel any particular thrill from seeing her car. People must fall in love in different ways. He didn't want to talk about her, either, the way Julius did. He just wanted—it sounded corny, but it was true—to do some great deed that would be worthy of her. But so far the only great deed he could think of was winning the science fair.

In first-period science, Ms. Gunderson again gave the class time to work on their projects. Most kids were working in groups of two or three, so all around the room they were busy pulling their desks together. Ethan sat alone. So did Julius. Ethan hoped some kids would invite Julius to join their group. No one did. He and Julius had worked together so many times, yet no one seemed to notice that today Julius's only partner had abandoned him.

Once again Ms. Gunderson circulated from group to group, talking over everyone's ideas. As she sat with Marcia's group, right next to him, Ethan stared at her instead of at the blank page on which he had written SCIENCE FAIR IDEAS so hopefully last night. Her hair was up, in a long braid twisted around her head. It made her look foreign—Swedish, maybe. She wore a purplish dress today, as long and swirly as her skirt had been yesterday.

She was standing up. She was turning away from Marcia's group. She was coming toward him. She was pulling up an empty chair next to his.

"Ethan," she said in her low voice.

She remembered his name.

Ethan tried to make his face look mature and intelligent, the thoughtful face of a future scientist.

"Have you had a chance to think any more about the science fair project?" she asked him.

Only every minute since nine-thirty yesterday morning.

Ethan nodded. He laid his arm over his blank paper,

to hide its blankness. "I have a few ideas I'm working on, but they're still pretty rough."

Ms. Gunderson didn't get up to go on to the next group. She sat patiently. Her expectant silence invited Ethan to say more.

"I sort of wanted to do something . . . different," Ethan said finally.

"Different?"

"My mom has this book on science fair projects— it's a library book, really—but I didn't want to do another one of the experiments from the book." *I want to do an experiment that will win the Nobel Prize.* He didn't say it. He couldn't meet her eyes.

"That's wonderful, Ethan," Ms. Gunderson said softly. "I've found that 'different' experiments are usually the best. And I know it's a lot harder to come up with something of your own. I think the secret is to start with a problem that interests you. Start by making a list of some things you really care about."

"Um, sports, I guess."

As soon as he had said it, he hated himself. Sports! He sounded as idiotic as Barnett yesterday, stammering about "wires and stuff." He wanted to sound like Einstein or Sir Isaac Newton, not like a dumb sports nut—worse, a dumb sports nut who wasn't even good at sports.

"Ethan."

He made himself look up, but not directly at her face.

"The human body in motion is a fascinating subject for science. There are hundreds—thousands—of exciting scientific questions that have to do with sports. I know you'll find one that will make a wonderful science fair project."

She smiled at him and he smiled back, catching her enthusiasm like a softball dropped from the sky overhead into his waiting glove.

Then she was gone, off to Lizzie's desk. Lizzie was the only kid besides Ethan and Julius who was working alone.

Could you win a Nobel Prize for discovering something about sports? Ethan didn't know. But he was determined to find out.

During study hall, Ethan made some more entries in *Life Isn't Fair: A Proof*. If he kept going at this rate, before the year was out he would have written a book longer than *A Tale of Two Cities*.

Tuesday, January 28. In art class, everybody's pots were fired in a kiln. Ethan Winfield's pot was the only one that cracked. Ms. Neville told him, "These things happen."

Tuesday, January 28. During math class, Ethan Winfield's PAL partner wrote a whole entire poem called "Ode to Winter."

That night the Winfields had spaghetti and meatballs for dinner. Ethan was starving. Being in love seemed to give him an appetite.

"How was school today?" Ethan's mother asked.

"Fine," Peter said.

"Fine," Ethan said.

"Just 'fine'? Nothing wonderful? Nothing terrible?"

Peter shook his head. Ethan did, too.

Tonight Peter gave in first. "At practice after school this afternoon, Coach Stevens took me aside and told me—well, he does want Coach McIntosh to know that I'll be coming up to Summit High next year and, you know, to be kind of on the lookout for me."

"That's great, son," Ethan's dad said.

"I just wish I were taller," Peter said.

Peter wished *he* were taller? If Ethan could ever be five foot six, he would never again ask for anything.

"You're still growing," Ethan's mom said. "Both of you are still growing."

"How's Edison Blue?" Ethan asked, to change the subject.

"The same. Today Troy Downing brought in his pet dog, Winkles, for sharing time, and Edison told Troy that Winkles was *not* a dog. The more Troy insisted that Winkles *was* a dog, the more Edison insisted that he was *not* a dog. The two of them actually came to blows over it."

"Who won?" Peter asked.

"Well, I put a stop to the punching right away. But Edison never backed down. Don't go away, there's apple crisp for dessert."

As she was serving the crisp, she said to Peter, "You're not worried about Friday night, are you?"

"Not really," Peter said. "Maybe a little bit."

"Don't worry," she told him. "Just play the way you always do."

In other words, Ethan thought, just be perfect. And of course Peter would be, as always, and Coach McIntosh would be astonished by Peter's wonderfulness, as all grownups always were, and next year Peter would be as big a star in high school as he had been all through middle school. At least Ethan wouldn't have to witness it all firsthand.

Five

By Wednesday, Monday's snow had mostly melted. There was still enough snow in shady patches for Ethan and Julius to use in a quick snowball fight on the way home from school, but most of the lawns were bare.

Julius had to go to his orthodontist appointment, so they couldn't have an after-school meeting of Losers, Inc. Instead, Ethan shot baskets in his driveway all alone. He tried lay-up after lay-up until the muscles in his arms and shoulders began to ache. It was a good kind of ache, the satisfying soreness of muscles training themselves to do what they were supposed to do.

Then Ethan dribbled up and down the driveway as fast and hard as if he were driving down the court with the other team's guards in hot pursuit. The impact of his hand against the ball, the rhythm of the ball rebounding from the pavement, the tingling warmth in his forearms—it all felt great.

The ball bounced obediently under his hand, as if some force in the ball were responding directly to the force in his cupped fingers. Bounce. Bounce. Bounce. Bounce. Ethan felt like a bouncing machine, programmed to keep on bouncing the ball in the same unchanging rhythm forever. Bounce. Bounce. What made a basketball bounce the way it did? Why was it bouncier than a soccer ball, even though both were about the same size and shape? And those tiny little super-balls. Why did they bounce so hard and so high?

Ethan caught the ball on its next up-bounce. He had it! He had the question for his science fair project. He would test all different kinds of balls, bouncing on all different kinds of surfaces, to try to find out which balls bounced the highest and why. He knew it wouldn't win a Nobel Prize, but he had thought it up all by himself, and it had come out of a real question that really mattered to him, just as Ms. Gunderson had said it should. He could hear her voice right now, telling him, "Why, Ethan, what an original idea! I knew you'd come up with something wonderful!"

On Thursday morning, they didn't have class time to work on their projects, but Ethan made himself go up to her after class. She was wearing a tight-fitting top, the kind that dancers wear, and the same skirt she had worn on the first day Ethan had ever seen her. Her hair was down, held back from her face by two glistening silver barrettes.

"I have kind of an idea for my science fair project," he told her.

"What is it?" she asked, as if there were nothing in the world she wanted to know more.

And when he told her, sure enough, she said, "Ethan! It's perfect for you. I knew your interest in sports would lead you to something wonderful."

Even Peer-Assisted Learning couldn't spoil Ethan's happiness. He felt so good that for the first time he tried to pay attention to Lizzie's long, breathless explanations of the day's new batch of math problems.

During study hall that day, Ethan actually studied. He wasn't going to be able to finish all 422 pages of *A Tale of Two Cities* in fourteen days unless he forced himself to read at least 30 pages—30 whole entire pages—every single day, including weekends. He was up to page 90 so far. If he had picked the 103-page book about a dog that Julius had found for him, he would be almost finished by now. Except that he wouldn't have started it yet. He and Julius always put off reading their book-report books until the night before the book reports were due.

A Tale of Two Cities wasn't the best book Ethan had ever read, but it wasn't the worst, either. It took place during the French Revolution, in the 1700s. Once Ethan realized that Madame Guillotine was a special machine for cutting off heads, the story became considerably more interesting. They were a pretty bloodthirsty bunch, those French Revolutionaries.

Ethan could tell that his reading during study hall annoyed Julius. Sitting next to him, Julius fidgeted. He started another batch of doodles of Ms. Gunderson. The point on his pencil broke. He sighed heavily. Then he trudged off to sharpen his pencil.

When Julius returned to their table, he whispered to Ethan, "You're really going to read the whole thing?"

Ethan nodded. He *was* going to read the whole thing, every single, solitary page. He didn't know how to explain his determination to Julius.

"I have to." He heard Ms. Leeds's voice again in his head: "I have to say that it is *very* disturbing . . ." But he didn't feel like letting Julius see how much the teacher's comments had bothered him. Instead he said, "It's my revenge against the Lizard. When she sees I'm reading a longer book than she did, she'll die. She always reads the longest book of anyone in the class. This time she won't."

"It's not worth it," Julius said. "I wouldn't read 422 pages to stop someone from blowing up the world."

The librarian, Ms. Dworkin, called over to them. "Boys, this is supposed to be *quiet, independent* study time." Across the room, Alex Ryan snorted. Alex loved it when anybody else got yelled at.

Ethan read for a few more minutes. When he looked up from his book, he saw Lizzie, at the next table, watching him. *Would* she be jealous when she saw he was reading a longer book than hers? No, Lizzie didn't seem competitive in that way.

The bell rang. Ethan was stuffing *A Tale of Two Cities* into his backpack when he heard Lizzie's voice beside him.

"You're reading *Dickens*?"

Ethan nodded warily.

"I *love* Dickens. Have you read *Great Expectations*? Or *Oliver Twist*? *Oliver Twist* is my favorite. I've read it twice. I cried both times when Bill Sikes murdered Nancy, even though she loved him so much. I can't believe someone else in our class is reading Dickens."

To his dismay, Ethan found himself walking down the hall to English with Lizzie by his side, still talking, talking, talking.

"I didn't know you were such a big reader, Ethan," Lizzie said. "I guess because your book-report books are always so short. But *length* isn't what matters in a book. I love a lot of short books, too. Or look at poetry. A poem can be any length. There are millions of wonderful poems that are just a few lines long. Like Emily Dickinson's poems. She can say more in two lines than most people can say in a hundred pages. What part are you up to in *A Tale of Two Cities*?"

They had reached the English room.

"Page 97," Ethan said. "I think the bell is going to ring."

He took his seat. Had anyone besides Julius seen him walking with the Lizard? He made himself look at Julius. The pity that shone from his friend's eyes was embarrassing, but in a way comforting, too.

"If I didn't know better," Julius said in a voice low enough that no one else could hear, "I'd say the Lizard likes you."

"She likes me," Ethan said dully.

"I guess it backfired," Julius said. "Your revenge against Lizzie. But at least you can stop reading *A Tale of Two Cities* now."

Ethan didn't know what to say. "Yeah, well, but at this point, I might as well go ahead and finish it. I mean, I've already read 97 pages. It'd be a shame to waste them."

Julius just shook his head. But Ethan hadn't been reading *A Tale of Two Cities* to irritate Lizzie. Or even to prove something to Ms. Leeds. He had been reading it to be worthy of Grace Gunderson. Even if she never knew he had read it, he was reading it for her.

On Friday afternoon, classes were canceled during eighth period for a school-wide pep rally in the gym. Red Rocks Middle School was West Creek's biggest rival in every sport, and both boys' basketball teams were going into tonight's game undefeated. It would be the game of the season.

As he walked to the pep rally with Julius, Ethan gathered data for another entry in *Life Isn't Fair: A Proof*:

Friday, January 31. On the way to the pep rally, three different kids asked Ethan Winfield, "Are you really Peter Winfield's brother?"

When the team came running out into the gym, the kids in the bleachers went wild. The cheerleaders led the crowd in a cheer for each player: "Pisani, Pisani, he's our man! If he can't do it, Winfield can! Winfield, Winfield, he's our man! If he can't do it, nobody can!"

Ethan's throat was hoarse from yelling. He had cheered as loudly as he could for all the others, but he tried to cheer even more loudly when it was Peter's turn. He felt ashamed of the disloyal thought he had had the other night at dinner. Peter had to play well tonight. The West Creek Bears had to win. And Ethan couldn't wait to see it happen.

At the game, Ethan sat high in the bleachers again, this time with his mom and dad. Lots of his classmates were there: Julius was sitting with Alex and David; Marcia was in a group of the most popular sixth-grade girls. Ethan didn't see the Lizard. Lizzie never went to any of the games.

Some of the teachers were there, too. Ethan searched every section of bleachers for Ms. Gunderson. He half wanted to find her and half hoped he wouldn't. If she saw Peter leading the team to victory tonight, she would never again think Ethan was wonderful. But she wasn't there. She was probably out with her friends from the university. Or with her boyfriend. There was no way someone as beautiful as she was wouldn't have a boyfriend. Ethan tried not to think what he would be like. Tall, most likely. Definitely taller than four feet ten and a half inches.

When the team came running out of the locker room to start the game, Ethan jumped to his feet along with everyone else to yell a welcome. Both of his parents were yelling, too. Ethan got a kick out of watching his parents at Peter's games. His dad, so quiet at home, had the loudest voice in the gym. At least it sounded that way to Ethan. No one had a more booming cheer when West Creek scored, or a more heartrending groan when they missed. Ethan's mother, on the other hand, could hardly bear to watch the game. Whenever Peter had the ball, she would close her eyes and wait for the roar of the crowd to tell her she could open them. Ethan suspected that when he, Ethan, had played junior league soccer back in elementary school, she had kept her eyes closed most of the time.

The first half of the game was a close one, ending 28–24, with West Creek in the lead. Peter had scored 10 of West Creek's points, making him the team's highest scorer for the half. But in the second half, the West Creek Bears couldn't seem to do anything right. Peter missed three shots in a row and got called for a foul against a Red Rocks player. With less than a minute left in the final quarter, the Bears were behind 42–38. West Creek would have to make two baskets in the next fifty seconds, or go down in defeat. And Ethan was painfully conscious that somewhere in the stands

Coach McIntosh from the high school was watching both teams play, scouting to see which players would be the high school's future stars.

All Ethan heard from his father was groans now. His mother hadn't been watching the game since the final quarter began. Coach Stevens called a time-out. Would he replace Peter with another forward? Ethan didn't think he could stand it if Peter had to sit out the rest of the game on the bench in disgrace. But Peter ran back in with his teammates, looking grim.

The coach's talking-to must have helped. West Creek scored: 42–40. Before Red Rocks could recover, Peter stole the ball from one of their forwards and made a quick lay-up, tying the score. Everyone in the gym was standing now, screaming. There were only ten seconds left on the clock. Ethan glanced at the scoreboard. Red Rocks was out of time-outs.

The Red Rocks guard threw a wobbly pass in from under the basket. Nine seconds. Eight. The ball rolled free, and Peter dove for it, along with two Red Rocks players. Ethan couldn't tell exactly what was happening in the next few seconds of pushing and grabbing.

The referee's whistle blew. Was the foul Peter's—his second foul of the evening? But the referee called it against Red Rocks.

"Right!" Ethan's father shouted, punching his fist in the air.

Peter took his place at the free-throw line. He had two chances now to win the game for his team. The gym had become eerily quiet. How did Peter take the pressure of having to make his best shot with everyone watching him? Ethan loved basketball, but he didn't think he could stand being a basketball star. He'd hate having hundreds and hundreds of people holding their breath, staring at him.

Ethan's mother had hidden her face in his father's shoulder. Ethan wanted to bury his own face in his father's other shoulder, but he kept his eyes on Peter.

Was it wrong to pray for someone to make a basket? Ethan couldn't help himself. *Dear God, let Peter make it. Let Peter make it.*

The ball soared through the air, teetered on the rim, and fell away. No score. A collective moan of disappointment came from the crowd.

Peter bounced the ball twice on the free-throw line. Then, carefully, he took aim. Ethan stopped breathing. The ball swished cleanly through the hoop. 43–42.

No one watched the last two seconds of the game. The crowd drowned out the buzzer announcing that the game was over and West Creek had won. Ethan's father had tears in his eyes. His mother was blowing her nose.

Ethan's chest was bursting with relief and pride in Peter, together with a secret pain. The wild and joyous cheers resounding through the gym were for his brother; they would always be for his brother. They would never be for him.

Six

As soon as Ethan reached school on the Monday after the game, he could tell that something was wrong.

It started when Alex Ryan greeted him on the playground. "Oh, Eeee-than!" Alan screeched in a high, piercing voice. "Oh, my darling Eeee-than!"

Alex's fake display of lovey-doveyness could mean only one thing. The others had found out that the Lizard had a crush on him. Lizzie had liked him for a whole week now; Ethan should probably consider himself lucky to have had her crush escape public notice this long. One thing about Lizzie, after all: She was definitely noticeable.

Ethan had learned from past experience that teasing goes away fastest if you ignore it. So he acted as if he hadn't heard Alex. He took out the basketball that he had somehow managed to cram into his backpack and dribbled it a couple of times on the blacktop. Then he ran for a lay-up. He missed, of course.

"Nice one," Alex called out.

Then Alex crossed the blacktop to where Ethan was still dribbling the ball.

"I have a poem for you, Eeee-than. I wrote it just for you."

It was much harder to ignore someone at close range, but Ethan tried. He pretended he was bouncing the basketball for his science experiment. Bounce. Bounce. Scientists were able to concentrate on their work despite all kinds of rude distractions. Like Pierre and Marie Curie. Ethan was sure they had concentrated on discovering radium even when others were teasing them about liking each other.

"Roses are red. Violets are blue," Alex chanted. "Lizards are green. And one loves you."

Ethan kept on bouncing the ball, but now, to his annoyance, the ball seemed to echo the rhythm of Alex's ridiculous rhyme. LIZ-ards are GREEN. And ONE loves YOU.

Should Ethan keep on ignoring Alex? Should he laugh to show that he could take a joke, that he thought Lizzie's crush on him was every bit as dumb as Alex thought it was? The real meanness in Alex's voice made it hard to laugh. That was the thing about Alex. His teasing always had a mean edge.

"Ethan! Here!" It was Julius, holding up his arms for

the ball. Relieved, Ethan threw the ball to him. Julius actually caught it.

"Hey, Julius," Alex said, "did you know that Ethan has a girlfriend?"

Ethan forgot his plan to stay calm and collected. "I do not!"

"Ethan and Lizzie sitting in a tree!" Alex said. "K-I-S-S-I-N-G!"

"Did you make that up yourself, Alex?" Julius said. "You really are one witty guy. A guy with your original sense of humor shouldn't be hanging around in Colorado; you should be off in California writing sitcoms for TV."

Alex glared at him. Julius bounce-passed the ball to Ethan. Ethan caught it and then, to his grateful surprise, made the next two baskets.

During homeroom, Ethan wondered exactly how the others had found out that Lizzie liked him. Marcia had probably told them. She was the kind of girl who loved to know a secret about somebody that she could tell to somebody else. He remembered how she had snatched back the poem she had shown him last week, most likely so she could have the pleasure of showing it around. Not that Lizzie ever tried to hide any of her poems. She scribbled in her notebook in full view of the whole world. More than once, Ethan had seen Marcia standing right behind Lizzie, reading over her shoulder.

One thing was clear, though. If Lizzie's crush had been a secret last week, it was a secret no longer. When Ethan walked into science class, a couple of the guys in the back of the room made loud kissing noises. On the chalkboard someone had written, in an oversized heart: E.W. + L.A. Ethan wanted to erase it before Ms. Gunderson saw it, but he would only call attention to himself by going up to the board.

Ms. Gunderson ended up erasing the heart herself, after the bell rang. Ethan hoped she didn't think he was the E.W. who supposedly loved L.A. For the truth was that E.W. loved G.G.

In art class, Ethan found a poem waiting for him on his desk.

To Ethan, My True Love

I love you, dear Ethan.
You are my hero.
Even though sometimes
You act like a weirdo.

I love you, dear Ethan,
Even though your ears stick out.
I love you, even though
Your nose looks like a snout.

It was signed: "Your loveress forever, Lizzie Archer."
Who had written it? Definitely not Lizzie. It wasn't

Lizzie's handwriting, or her style. Was it Alex? Or someone else? It must have been Alex. It would be too depressing if all the guys except Julius turned against him.

Ethan reached up and felt his ears. He didn't think they stuck out. And he was almost sure that there was nothing wrong with his nose, except for a few freckles. Did he act like a weirdo? He couldn't think of any weird things he had done lately, but maybe if the Lizard liked you, that was proof enough that you were weird.

On the way to third-period math, Ethan prayed. *Dear God, please don't let this be a day for Peer-Assisted Learning.*

But God seemed to listen better to prayers about Peter. As soon as the bell rang, Mr. Grotient said, "Let's begin with Peer-Assisted Learning. I want to make sure you have enough time to get a good start on studying for your next exam."

The others began the familiar pushing and shoving of desks.

"Oh, Eeee-than!" Alex called over to him. "Lizzie is waiting for you!"

David Barnett joined in. "Oh, Lizzz-ie! Come to Eeee-than!"

Ethan didn't move. The chorus of "Eeee-than!" and "Lizzz-ie!" continued.

"Boys! Is there some problem?" Mr. Grotient finally seemed to notice that there was a disturbance in the room. Today his bow tie and suspenders were both fire-engine red. "Please move your desks *quickly* and *quietly*."

Ethan couldn't move his. He just couldn't. He waited for Lizzie to move hers. She didn't budge, either.

"Ethan, Lizzie, get moving," Mr. Grotient said. "Let me remind you that the next exam is going to determine half your grade for this marking period."

After one of the longest minutes that Ethan had ever known, Lizzie slowly moved her desk—not right next to his this time, but close enough to satisfy Mr. Grotient.

"Do you want to review chapter seven or go on to chapter eight?" Lizzie asked in a strangled voice.

Ethan didn't reply.

"Chapter seven?"

Ethan still didn't speak.

"Okay, remember how on the first problem, *x* was in the denominator?" Lizzie's voice was more steady now. She was at her best when she could be the perfect student, smarter than everyone who laughed at her.

Ethan let her talk, not that he could have stopped her. But he didn't say anything to her, not one word, for the rest of the period.

At lunch, Ethan hoped that he and Julius could sit by themselves and be ignored by the others. It would be nice to have a private meeting of Losers, Inc. But David and Alex plunked their trays down on Ethan's table, and a moment later Marcia joined them.

"Romeo, Romeo!" David said, with an exaggerated sigh. Marcia giggled.

"Have you kissed her yet?" Alex asked.

Ethan felt himself flushing with shame and fury.

"Have *you*?" Julius asked Alex. The question fell flat.

"Look," Ethan said. He felt he had to say it once and for all, clearly enough that the others could not possibly misunderstand him. "I do not—like—Lizzie." He couldn't bring himself to say the word *love*. "I have never liked Lizzie. I will never like Lizzie. In fact, if you want to know the truth, I hate Lizzie."

The others still looked unconvinced.

"It just so happens," Ethan said, "that I am violently allergic to lizards."

Barnett laughed then. Encouraged, Ethan said, "My doctor did tests. I'm allergic to anything that has scales and is slimy and writes poetry."

Marcia laughed, too. Ethan had won over two of them.

"I break out in big red hives all over my body if anyone reads a poem in my presence," Ethan went on.

"Lizzie wrote another one about you this morning," Marcia said. "It started out, 'Though your lips and mine may never meet . . .'"

"Help!" Ethan said. "I'm starting to break out!"

He was beginning to feel less desperate, though Alex

still refused to join in the laughter. Alex wanted to laugh *at* people, not with them.

"She really thinks her poems are good, too," Marcia said. "Like she's the next Shakespeare or something."

"You know what would be funny?" Alex said. "If we, like, pretended there was a contest. Like a big contest for writing poetry? We could put up signs and things. And when she entered it, we'd send her a letter saying she won. Only it would all be a joke."

"Dear Miss Archer," David said, using a fake-solemn voice. "It is my pleasure to inform you that you have just won first prize in the nation for your poem 'Love Song to Ethan.' "

Marcia snorted.

Ethan pretended to gag at the title of the poem. "Let's do it," he said loudly. He had to stop Lizzie from writing love poems about him for the whole class to see; he couldn't spend the rest of the year listening to a chorus of kissing sounds whenever he walked into a room. "It'd be easy. All we have to do is print up some flyers on somebody's computer."

"Where would we have people send the poems?" David asked. "It'll look kind of strange if it's one of our houses here in West Creek."

"We can use my cousin," Marcia said. "She lives in Washington, D.C. That'll make it look real official. The National Poetry Writing Contest, in the nation's capital."

"And then we'll tell her?" Julius asked. He sounded

uncomfortable. "That it's all a joke? When it's all over?"

"Yeah, after she's bragged about it to everybody," Alex said.

Julius didn't say anything else. Ethan knew Julius well enough to know what Julius was thinking: The plan was too mean.

The plan *was* too mean. Ethan had told the others that he hated Lizzie. But he didn't really hate *her*. He just hated being teased about her. He didn't want to hurt Lizzie. She would be so excited when she got the letter, so pleased and proud. Poetry was all Lizzie had. Well, poetry and long book reports and being good at math and having all the teachers love her. But she didn't have anything else. It would be a cruel thing to trick her this way. But she'd get over it. Maybe she wouldn't even believe the letter when she got it. Lizzie was smart, after all. And if she did believe it, well, then it would serve her right, in a way, for being so gullible.

It was easy for Julius to sit back and judge. Nobody was writing poems about *his* lips. If Ethan went along with the plan, it would save him from being the laughingstock of the sixth grade. No one could possibly think he was Lizzie's boyfriend now.

Seven

David and Alex had agreed to make the flyers for the poetry contest on David's computer. Ethan looked for them as he and Julius walked to homeroom on Tuesday morning. Sure enough, they were there, prominently displayed on the big bulletin board by the main office and on the Book News bulletin board outside the library. There was a school rule against posting any unauthorized notices on bulletin boards, but these flyers looked amazingly professional. No one could have guessed that they were made by sixth graders.

Would Lizzie see them? Did anybody ever actually look at a school bulletin board? Until this morning, Ethan never had. It was a flaw in the plan that none of them had considered. Ethan decided he'd better mention the flyers to Lizzie during Peer-Assisted Learning. He had to say something to her, anyway, after being so cold and silent all through class yesterday.

No one teased Ethan about Lizzie today. There were no hearts with his initials in them scrawled on any chalkboards, no annoying chants of "Eeee-than!" and "Lizzz-ie!" Ethan had never seen an episode of teasing end more quickly and completely.

In math class, Ethan pulled his desk promptly over to Lizzie's, without waiting for her to move her desk.

"Um—Lizzie?" It was the first time he had ever spoken to her without her speaking first. She looked up, her thin, freckled face flushing with pleasure.

"I don't know if you saw, but there's a flyer on the bulletin board. It's for, like, a poetry contest—and, well, I know you write poetry, and . . ." His voice trailed off.

"A contest? No, I didn't see it, but I *love* contests. I enter them all the time. I never win, but you have to keep trying, right? I read somewhere that some famous writers have their books rejected twenty or thirty times before they're finally published. And you definitely can't win if you don't enter." Lizzie opened her math book. "It was nice of you to tell me," she said softly.

Now Ethan was blushing. Of course, it wasn't nice of him to tell her about the contest. It was probably the single meanest thing he had ever done in his life.

He felt less mean, or at least less bad about being mean, when Marcia came up to him at lunch.

"I copied this out of Lizzie's notebook when she was getting changed for gym," Marcia said.

This time Ethan held the poem firmly so that Marcia couldn't snatch it back.

To Ethan

I will love thee in the winter,
When the ice and snow lie deep.
I will love thee in the spring,
When the budding willows weep.
I will love thee in the summer,
When the sun burns hot and bold.
I will love thee in the fall,
When the aspen leaves turn gold.
I will love thee all year long.
Love eternal is my song.

One season of love from the Lizard was terrible enough. Her eternal love was something no one could be expected to bear.

During study hall, Ethan read ten more pages of *A Tale of Two Cities*. He had kept on schedule all weekend, so that he was up to page 260 now. He had begun thinking of each page read as an offering to lay at Ms. Gunderson's feet. Two hundred and sixty offerings to lay before her black ballet-type shoes, the ones with the long, skinny straps that wound around her ankles.

He was becoming a faster reader, too. When he closed *A Tale of Two Cities* on page 260, there were still a few minutes left in study hall. Ethan closed his eyes as if he were sleeping—next to him, Julius *was* asleep—and thought some more about the science fair. It was three weeks away, but he wasn't going to leave his experiment to the last week, not this time.

He'd have to get all different kinds of balls and figure out what they were made of. Maybe the library had a book on balls. The school librarian, Ms. Dworkin, was nice, even if she yelled at Ethan and Julius sometimes for talking. Maybe she could help Ethan find out which balls were made of what.

Then he'd test them by bouncing them on various surfaces—hard, soft, rough, smooth—and measuring the results. He'd have to make sure he bounced them all the same way every time, though. That would be the tricky part. Maybe he could rig up some kind of machine that could bounce balls uniformly.

After school, Ethan went to Julius's house. Julius lived about a half mile from Ethan. It was an easy walk or bike ride now that they were older, but Ethan re-membered how far it had seemed when they had first become friends, back in second grade. Back then Ethan's parents had thought he was too little to go that far from home on his own, and Peter had had to take him to Julius's, riding his big bike next to Ethan's small one.

It was hard to believe that he and Julius had been friends for so many years. Even in second grade, they

66

•

had been losers together. Ethan remembered that the class had been assigned that year to build a shoe-box diorama for Presidents' Day. He and Julius had used real maraschino cherries on the cardboard cherry tree that George Washington was chopping down in their diorama, and a colony of ants had found them.

"What do you want to eat?" Julius asked after they had shed their coats and boots in the mud room. "There's ice cream, or we could do a frozen pizza."

"Pizza," Ethan said. Ice cream reminded him too much of Julius's science fair project. He didn't know if he should mention the project or not. Neither Ethan nor Julius had mentioned the science fair to each other during the past week. But it seemed strange not to even *talk* about their projects.

"Speaking of ice cream," Ethan said, trying to sound casual, "how's the science project coming?"

"Great," Julius said. He sounded as if he meant it, almost as if he were bragging. But Julius never bragged.

"Are you still doing it on ice cream?"

"Uh-huh. Grace thinks it's a fantastic idea. She said that everybody makes all these claims all the time about fat-free foods and how terrific they taste, and it's a wonderful idea to really go out and test them."

Julius's confident use of her first name startled Ethan. It was true that sometimes he himself thought of her as Grace. The name suited her so perfectly. But he would never have said her name out loud to anyone else, as if he had a *right* to use it. And he hadn't thought the ice cream idea sounded all that wonderful. It had sounded to him like an excuse to get your parents to buy a lot of ice cream.

Ethan waited to see if Julius would ask him what he had decided to do his science project on. He wasn't sure he wanted to tell Julius. For the first time ever, he felt as if he were competing against his best friend to be the best, rather than competing with him against everybody else, to be the worst. However fantastic Ms. Gunderson thought Julius's project was, Ethan wanted her to think his project was even better. He could hardly be a member in worse standing of Losers, Inc.

But Julius didn't ask, and even though Ethan hadn't wanted him to ask, when Julius didn't, Ethan found himself feeling hurt. You'd think best friends would at least take an interest in each other's projects, even if they had decided not to work together.

"I have an idea," Julius said then, as he slid the frozen pizza into the oven. The strained moment had passed, and Julius sounded like himself again. "Let's look Grace up in the phone book and see where she lives."

The idea, simple as it was, had never occurred to Ethan. He hadn't had as much practice at being in love as Julius had. For some reason, he almost didn't want to know where Ms. Gunderson lived, in her life outside of school. He felt strangely nervous as Julius opened the Metro Area directory.

"Here she is," Julius said, pouncing with his finger halfway down the page. "Gunderson, G. 1250 Alfalfa Lane. 555-8537."

Ethan took the phone book and stared at the listing. It made her seem so . . . real, as if she wasn't just a figment of his imagination. It was reassuring and yet disappointing, too. Rapunzel shouldn't have an ordinary street address.

"If I called her up, what would I say?" Julius asked. "I used to call Stephanie sometimes, but all I did was hang up when I heard her voice."

"I don't know," Ethan said. If *he* called her, what would *he* say?

The pizza was ready, so the boys fell silent and devoured it.

"We could ride over to Alfalfa Lane and see where she lives," Julius said after they'd finished eating.

Ethan knew he would be sorry for what he said next. "Okay."

Alfalfa Lane, it turned out, was only a mile away. Number 1250 was a large, red-brick garden-apartment complex. Ethan had passed it many times, but he had never ridden through it.

"Now what?" Ethan asked. "Which apartment is hers?"

"I guess we'll have to look at mailboxes," Julius said.

Outside each block of apartments stood a large bank of mailboxes with the names of the residents posted on each one. Ethan and Julius started with the A-block apartments and went in alphabetical order from there. They finally found her in the H's: H16.

"At least she wasn't in the Z's," Julius said.

Ethan felt his heart pounding as if he had just ridden his bike over the Continental Divide. What if she saw them? What if she was with someone? Like, a guy?

"Let's get out of here," Ethan said. "She could show up any minute."

He pushed off on his bike. Julius could hang around as long as he wanted. Ethan was leaving.

Then he saw her, getting out of the small silver Honda that had just pulled into the parking lot. She was alone. So God had answered one prayer even before Ethan had a chance to ask it.

"Hello, Julius. And Ethan!" Her voice was full of pleasure. "I didn't know you boys lived at the Meadows."

"We don't," Julius said, like a dope.

Ethan had to say something then. "We were just riding by." As if anybody would take a bike ride all through somebody else's apartment complex and just happen by coincidence to end up at her door.

"Well, it's a beautiful day for a ride," Ms. Gunderson said. "It feels just like spring."

She went into the entrance for apartment H16. Ethan

and Julius gazed after her until she disappeared from sight.

"She knows we were looking for her place," Julius said. He looked sheepish, but a bit pleased with himself, too. "The way she looked at me. She knows."

But it had been Ethan she had looked at before turning to go inside.

"She knows," Ethan agreed miserably. She definitely knew.

By Saturday morning, Ethan had collected ten different balls to test, and he had found a library book on balls in the children's room at the public library. It was actually a book for little kids, full of pictures, but it had lots of information on balls. After *A Tale of Two Cities*, it was a relief to be reading a book with only 64 pages.

He was still reading his daily quota of Dickens. He would be finished easily by the time he had to give his book report on Monday, though he still had to come up with something to say in the report. Ms. Leeds would expect more than "I read this whole book. It has 422 pages." But somewhere in his report, Ethan was going to work in, in a casual, offhand way, the number of pages. He couldn't wait to see Ms. Leeds's face when he did.

When Ethan came downstairs for breakfast, he had *A Tale of Two Cities* in his hand. Peter was up already, back from an early morning run, even though he had been out late last night at an away basketball game. Peter and their mother were morning people; Ethan and their father weren't.

"What's the book?" Peter asked. "Every time I see you now, you've got your nose in some book."

Ethan held it up, keeping his finger on page 367.

Peter looked impressed. Ethan made a mental note: On Saturday, February 8, at 10:07 a.m., Peter Winfield saw the book his brother, Ethan, was reading and looked genuinely impressed.

"How'd you get started on Dickens?" Peter asked.

"I don't know. I just thought I'd try a long book for a change."

"Hey, I just remembered something," Peter said. "This is funny. When I was in sixth grade, one time *I* read a really long book, the longest one in the class. Is this for one of Leeds's famous book reports? Mine was, too. What was it? That's right, *The Yearling*. It was a great book. A really great book. If you do another long book, read *The Yearling*."

"How long was it?" For some reason, Ethan had to know.

"I don't remember. Three hundred, four hundred pages. And sad. It's the saddest book I ever read."

"*A Tale of Two Cities* is sad, too." Were all long books sad? You'd think that after someone had read four hundred pages, the least he'd deserve was a happy ending. "Do you have it here? *The Yearling*?"

"No. It was from the library. What do you want to make for dinner tonight? Maybe Tex-Mex burgers, with salsa and guacamole? Tell Mom I went over to Josh's house to study for the math test. What about you? What're you doing?"

"I guess I'll go to the library. There's something I need to look up."

At the library, Ethan found *The Yearling* listed in the computer catalog. It was by Marjorie Kinnan Rawlings, shelved upstairs with the adult books.

There it was. It looked long, all right, longer than *A Tale of Two Cities*. It was definitely a fatter book, but maybe it was just printed on thicker paper.

Ethan made himself flip to the last page to check the page number: 400. Twenty-two pages shorter than *A Tale of Two Cities*.

He grinned like a fool at everybody he passed all the way home.

Eight

Monday, February 10. The bulletin board outside
the gym had two enormous pictures of Peter Winfield on it from Friday's basketball game. In gym
class Coach Stevens picked six guys to go to a special weekend basketball camp. Ethan Winfield was
not one of them.

Monday, February 10. Whoever invented alphabetical order? Every single time every single teacher
starts with A last names and ends with Z ones. Is it
just a coincidence that the president and vice president of Losers, Inc., both have last names from
the end of the alphabet?

Ethan was sitting in Ms. Leeds's sixth-period English
class, waiting for the stragglers to come in from study
hall and scribbling a couple of quick entries in *Life Isn't*

Fair: A Proof. He had been so busy lately bouncing balls and reading Dickens that he had gotten behind in his record keeping. And these days fewer unfair things seemed to be happening in his immediate vicinity. Or maybe he was just too preoccupied with the rest of his life to notice them.

It was book-report day, and Ethan knew that Ms. Leeds would start with Lizzie, as all teachers always started with Lizzie, and she'd get to Ethan and Julius if there was time, which there probably wouldn't be, since there were twenty-four kids in the class, and Lizzie could easily fill half a class period all by herself. Ethan looked down again at the page he had written on *A Tale of Two Cities.* If he had to wait till tomorrow to get his report over with, he didn't think he could stand it. Especially this time, when his report was practically guaranteed to astonish everybody, most of all Ms. Leeds.

The bell rang. Ms. Leeds looked up from her cluttered desk. She was a small, gray-haired woman who smiled so much that her face had frozen into a perpetually smiling expression.

"Let's get started right away," Ms. Leeds said. "I want to make sure we hear as many book reports as possible today. Lizzie, what do you have to share with us?"

Lizzie came to the front of the room. Most kids read their reports from a sheet of paper; some just mumbled something they thought of on the spot. Lizzie's book reports were always memorized. She clasped her hands behind her back, fixed her eyes somewhere on the ceiling, and let loose her usual torrent of words.

"I read a *wonderful* book called *Jane Eyre*, by Charlotte Brontë. It was written in 1847, but the characters in the book are so real that you feel as if they're living today. When I read this book, I felt as if *I* were Jane Eyre, a lonely, friendless orphan girl sent away to a cold, cruel boarding school where all the other girls despise her."

As Ethan had predicted, Lizzie's report was long. Many sad and terrible things had happened to Jane Eyre, and Lizzie apparently felt she had to describe each one in detail. Lizzie always loved the books in her book reports, but she seemed to love this one extra much. Maybe it was because she and Jane Eyre were a lot alike. Nobody liked either of them.

Finally Lizzie finished.

"David Barnett," Ms. Leeds called, still smiling.

B, C, D, E, F, G . . . Why did the alphabet have to have so many letters in it?

David started reluctantly toward the front of the room. To his own surprise, Ethan put up his hand.

"Ethan?"

"I was just wondering—do we always have to go in alphabetical order? Every time?"

Ms. Leeds kept on smiling her same smile. "Why, no.

Not at all. Would you like to proceed in a different way today?"

It wasn't as if Ethan was exactly eager for his turn; he was just so tired of being last. Though maybe he *was* looking forward to his report today. "I guess so," he said.

"Well, suppose today we go in *reverse* alphabetical order. Yes, I think that would be quite a refreshing change. Julius, why don't you go next?"

David flashed Ethan a jubilant grin. Ethan knew that David hadn't finished his book yet and was sitting with it open on his desk in the back of the room, trying to turn the pages without Ms. Leeds's seeing.

Julius glared at Ethan. Julius never minded bringing up the rear as the only Z in the entire school. He had once said to Ethan, "The way I look at it, this increases the odds that a tornado or an earthquake or a nuclear bomb will strike before I have to go."

"Julius?"

Julius walked slowly to the front of the room. In an expressionless monotone, he read from his paper: "I read *A Boy and a Dog*, by Maxwell Crumbly. It is about a boy and a dog." The rest of Julius's report gave the plot of the book, but it didn't tell anything *about* the book. You could have boiled down Julius's report to two sentences: "The boy gets lost on a rafting trip. The dog finds him." At the end of the report, Julius read, "This was an okay book. I would recommend this book to boys who like dogs." And he crumpled up his paper to show that he was finished.

"Does anyone have any questions for Julius about the book he selected?" Ms. Leeds asked. Her smile was somewhat less bright. No one raised a hand, so she asked, "Where does the story take place? Where is its setting?"

"Montana," Julius said. "On a river. The river is where they go rafting."

"Were there any other memorable characters in it? Besides the boy and the dog?"

"No," Julius said. "Oh, there's a bear. A grizzly bear. I guess I forgot to mention him."

Ms. Leeds didn't look completely satisfied, but she turned to Ethan. "Ethan, what about you? What do you have to share? I hope both you and Julius chose longer books this time. Remember, class, your book-report books must be at least one hundred pages. Julius, how long was *A Boy and a Dog*?"

"One hundred pages," Julius said. He held it up, open to page 100. In the back of the room, someone guffawed.

"Ethan?"

"I read *A Tale of Two Cities*, by Charles Dickens. It has 422 pages." Ethan tried to say it in a matter-of-fact tone, but he couldn't keep the glee out of his voice. Then he read his page. Like Julius's, it told mainly what the book was about. But the plot of *A Tale of Two Cities* was so complicated that it wasn't that easy to summarize in a page.

Basically, there were two guys who looked alike, Charles Darnay and Sydney Carton, and they were both in love with the same person, Lucie Manette, only Darnay got to marry her because he was a nobleman, plus a really wonderful person, and Sydney Carton was a super-loser. But then Darnay got arrested and condemned to death, and Sydney Carton helped him escape from prison and went off to be executed in his place, because he loved Lucie so much that he was willing to sacrifice himself so that she could be with the man she loved. Over the past two weeks, Ethan had found himself thinking of Lucie Manette as Grace Gunderson, and every once in a while he was Darnay, but mostly he was Sydney Carton.

"This is an excellent book," Ethan finished reading. "It teaches you about the French Revolution, which took place in the seventeen-nineties in the country of France. It is a good book if you like history or violence or exciting suspense. It is a love story, too, so some girls might like it. All in all, it is an excellent book."

Ethan started toward his seat. Relief mingled with pride. It was over now, the book *and* the report. If length counted for anything, he should get an A plus. His report hadn't been as long and flowery as Lizzie's, but it had been more interesting and informative than Julius's. Maybe he'd even get an A for the trimester. If

Ethan were the one giving out grades, anyone who read a book with 422 pages would get an A for the year.

But when he looked back at Ms. Leeds, he saw that she had stopped smiling. "Very nice," she said automatically. "Ethan, would you stay for a moment after class? There's something I need to ask you. All right, where were we? Timothy Williams, you're next."

As the rest of the kids droned on, the class became more and more fidgety. That was another problem with going last: It was hard to talk when everybody was passing notes and doodling on their book covers. Ethan wondered what Ms. Leeds wanted to say to him. Maybe she wanted to apologize to him for all those times they had gone in the usual order. Or for acting last time as if he were retarded for picking a short book.

The bell rang before Daniel Brotman and David Barnett had their turns. David was doing his best to look disappointed.

"First thing tomorrow, boys," Ms. Leeds told them.

Ethan put his notebook in his backpack and waited to see what Ms. Leeds had to say. Julius walked past him out to the hall without a word. Ethan wished he didn't know what Julius was thinking. But he did. *Some vice president of Losers, Inc., you are.*

"Hey, Julius, wait for me. I'll only be a minute," Ethan called after him.

Ethan didn't know if Julius would wait or not, but

then he saw his friend slide down to the floor just outside Ms. Leeds's door.

"Ethan." Ms. Leeds spoke stiffly. "I don't quite know how to say this to you. But I would rather you read the shortest possible book, as Julius did, rather than rely on plot summaries to pretend you read something you didn't read."

Ethan stared at her. "But I did read *A Tale of Two Cities*."

"Did you, Ethan?" Ms. Leeds's smile was horrible now. "Am I supposed to believe that one of my sixth-grade students read over four hundred pages in two weeks? A boy whose last book was on a third-grade reading level?"

"Lizzie reads long books." What else could Ethan say? He had no proof that he had read the book. Was he supposed to have made a videotape of all the dozens of hours he had spent reading it?

"Lizzie is an avid reader. Anyone can tell from the real passion in Lizzie's book reports that she lives in the worlds of the books she reads. Ethan, I am not going to penalize you this time. I know many students crib their reports from book jackets. But this was so blatant that I had to give you at least a warning."

"But I did read it," Ethan repeated stubbornly. He had a sudden, painful thought. He was willing to bet anything he owned that when Peter had read *The Yearling* for his book report in sixth grade, Ms. Leeds hadn't accused him of pretending to have read it. He had another entry for *Life Isn't Fair*, after all.

"I wish I could believe you," Ms. Leeds said. "All right, Ethan, you may go."

So much for Ethan's A plus. So much for reverse alphabetical order. So much for trying not to be a loser.

Suddenly Julius was by his side, pale, his eyes blinking the way they did whenever he was upset about something. "Ethan *did* read the book," Julius almost shouted. "The whole stinking book. I saw him. We all saw him. Go ask Ms. Dworkin what Ethan's been reading every day in study hall. Go ask your precious Lizzie. She saw him reading it last week. I told him he didn't have to read the whole thing, but he did. He read every single stinking page. All 422 of them."

Ethan didn't say anything. He had been all right a minute ago—furious, disgusted, sick to his stomach, but all right. Now he was afraid he might cry.

Julius had spoken with such angry intensity that no one could think he was lying to save his friend.

"I'm sorry, Ethan," Ms. Leeds said softly. She looked as if *she* was going to cry. The whole thing was becoming more embarrassing by the minute. "I shouldn't have doubted you. It was just that— Please accept my apology."

Ethan turned to go. It didn't matter, anyway.

Out in the hall, he and Julius hurried on to social

studies without speaking. Then, as they reached the classroom, Ethan made himself mutter, "Thanks."

Julius looked away. "I hope it was worth it," he said in a low voice. "Getting to go first. Reading the longest book. Telling everybody how *wonderful* it was. Do you know who you remind me of these days?"

Ethan didn't answer. He knew it wasn't Peter.

It was the Lizard.

Nine

Friday would be Valentine's Day. Ethan spent the rest of the week dreading its arrival. In elementary school, Valentine's Day had been no big deal. Everybody gave valentines to everybody else because all the mothers made sure they did. There was a party at school, with pink-frosted cupcakes and red punch. Ethan threw away his valentines as soon as he got home, first taking off any candy that was glued to them. Then he ate the candy. End of Valentine's Day.

Ethan didn't know what to expect from Valentine's Day in middle school. There wouldn't be a party this year. He knew that much. But this year there would be Lizzie. Ethan had never before had someone in love with him on Valentine's Day. The day was bound to call forth from her some loveress-like impulses.

And this year there was Grace. Ethan had never before been in love on Valentine's Day, either. Should he give her a valentine? It seemed to him that it would make a mockery out of his feelings to buy her one of those dumb, icky-sweet valentines in the card aisle at King Soopers—as if what he felt for her could be captured by a Hallmark card. But was Julius going to give her a valentine? If Julius did, then Ethan wanted to give her *something*. Maybe he could make her a valentine. That would have a little more meaning, at least, than buying one.

Thursday night he wandered into the family room. His father was watching a basketball game on cable with headphones, and his mother was reading a mystery novel.

"Um, Mom? You don't have any construction paper, do you?"

"It's in my crafts closet," she said. "Reams of it. What color do you need?"

Ethan didn't answer.

In the crafts closet he found a whole packet of red construction paper and took one sheet, hurrying to his room with it so that Peter wouldn't see. Then he had to go back downstairs to borrow the kitchen scissors. But just as he was about to cut the paper into a big red heart, he realized that he couldn't go through with it. He put the scissors back in the kitchen drawer and hid the red construction paper in the mess of papers on his desk. What he felt for Ms. Gunderson couldn't be put into a homemade valentine, either.

Friday morning came too soon. "Good morning! Happy Valentine's Day!" Ms. Romero read over the P.A. system at the start of homeroom. The principal's cheery words gave Ethan a sensation of nameless dread in the pit of his stomach. If his life were a horror movie, this was where the creepy music would begin to play.

On his way to science class, Ethan saw Marcia. She was wearing red heart-shaped earrings and a sweater with pink hearts embroidered on it. She had a sheaf of small white envelopes in her hand, obviously valentines. Ethan couldn't tell if they were all *for* her or *from* her—or all snatched away from somebody else.

"Ethan," she said when she saw him just outside the science room. She sorted through her pile of envelopes. "I have a valentine for you."

Ethan took it. Better a valentine from Marcia than a valentine from Lizzie.

"Guess what?" Marcia said, dropping her voice to a conspiratorial whisper. "She sent it in. Lizzie sent in a poem for the contest. My cousin called me from Washington last night to tell me that it came in the mail yesterday."

"What kind of poem?" Ethan meant: Was it a poem about him?

"It wasn't a love poem. It was about birds. I think it was called 'Snow Bird.' Not that it matters. It's going to win first prize anyway." Marcia laughed snidely.

Ethan gave a sort of laugh to echo hers, then went on into science class. But the more he thought about Lizzie's actually entering the contest, actually putting her poem so hopefully into the mail, the worse he felt. Nobody deserved to be laughed at for having a dream.

Ms. Gunderson wasn't wearing any special Valentine's Day clothes, but her hair was down. Maybe Ethan should have made her a valentine, after all. He wouldn't have had to sign his name to it, or anything. He just wanted to give her something. Like a single long-stemmed red rose. Why that idea popped into his head, Ethan didn't know. It would just be so perfect for her to glance down at her desk and find it lying there. She'd look up then, surprised, and her eyes would search the room, and when they fell on Ethan, he'd look away . . .

Ethan glanced down at his own desk. A folded sheet of paper lay there, with "To Ethan" written on it. It must be from Lizzie. When she had passed him in the hall on the way to class, she had looked even more intense and strange than usual, if that were possible. Her hair had seemed even redder and more electric.

Quickly Ethan stuck the paper, unread, into his backpack, next to Marcia's unopened valentine. Who had seen Lizzie deliver it? Alex? Marcia? Grace Gunderson?

Julius slipped into his seat next to Ethan. He leaned toward Ethan's desk and whispered, "I bought her a valentine. A real Hallmark valentine. It cost two-fifty."

"Did you give it to her yet?"

"I left it in her mailbox in the office. There were eleven other valentines there." Eleven dull blows at Ethan's heart. "I counted them. And two boxes of candy. One Whitman's and one Russell Stover."

More than ever, Ethan wished he had a rose to give her. His would have been the only rose.

"Good morning," Ms. Gunderson said. If Ethan had been blind, he would have loved her for her voice alone. "Today we are going to begin a series of experiments using the bunsen burners on the lab tables at the back of the room. Mr. O'Keefe has told me that this will be the first time you have used the bunsen burners this year, so I want to talk to you for a minute about bunsen burner safety."

The class moved to the lab tables. Ethan and Julius grabbed a lab table together in the back row. Marcia got stuck with Lizzie, right in front of them.

"When we use a bunsen burner, we always wear plastic safety goggles," Ms. Gunderson said. She picked up a pair and put them on. Everyone else did, too. No one giggled at how anyone else looked in their goggles, because Ms. Gunderson looked so grave and beautiful in hers.

"We always use wooden safety matches to light the burners," Ms. Gunderson said. She held up a box of wooden matches. "First you strike the match, and *then* you turn on the gas." She struck one, held it to the burner, and carefully turned on the gas. A bright flame appeared. In front of Ethan, Lizzie gave a small gasp, as if she had never seen fire before.

Ms. Gunderson extinguished her burner, then lit it again. "Does everyone understand the procedure?" she asked. "All right, I'd like each of you, one at a time, to light your burner for me, so I can check you on this."

Ethan heard Lizzie say to Marcia, "I *can't*. I've never lit a match before. I *can't*."

Marcia said, "*Anybody* can light a match."

When Ethan's turn came, he lit his burner smoothly. He wished Ms. Gunderson had asked him to do something more impressive, like walking barefoot over hot coals. Julius dropped the first match he lit. He gave a forced laugh, which came out more like a squeak. But he managed to light the burner on his second try.

Marcia lit her burner. Then it was Lizzie's turn. Lizzie's hand shook as she struck her match. Nothing happened. She struck it again. This time it burst into flame.

As everyone watched, Lizzie stood, paralyzed, staring at the burning match between her thumb and forefinger, making no move to turn on the gas.

"Lizzie, turn on the gas for your burner," Ms. Gunderson said quietly.

"Turn it on, stupid," Marcia hissed.

Lizzie didn't move. The flame on the match burned closer to her fingers. Still she stood there, motionless.

Ethan couldn't take it anymore. He leaned over

and blew out the match. Lizzie burst into hysterical tears.

"It's all right, Lizzie," Ms. Gunderson said. She sounded shaken herself. Probably nothing in her teacher training at the university had prepared her for Lizzie. "When we do our experiments, your lab partner can light your burner. David, you're next. Remember, match first, then gas."

Lizzie was still crying.

"What a spaz," Marcia said to anyone who was listening.

Ethan felt a sudden, unexpected pang of pity for Lizzie.

The rest of the bunsen burners were lit without any mishaps. Ms. Gunderson explained more safety procedures. Then the class period was finally over.

"Ethan," Ms. Gunderson called out over the ringing of the bell, "please stay for a minute."

This time Ethan didn't ask Julius to wait for him. But Julius did. Ethan tried to pretend that Julius wasn't there, lurking outside the science-room door. He turned to Ms. Gunderson. No one from the next class had come in yet. The two of them were alone.

"Ethan, that was quick thinking on your part," Ms. Gunderson said. "I have to admit that I wasn't expecting anyone to react quite as Lizzie did."

Ethan tried to shrug nonchalantly, but he could feel an idiotic grin spreading across his face.

"Lizzie is an unusual girl," Ms. Gunderson went on. "I know that some of the members of our class haven't been particularly kind to her. Thank you, Ethan, for not being one of them."

Ms. Gunderson smiled at him. Ethan smiled back. Other students began coming in. The moment was over.

Ethan met Julius outside in the hall.

"Well?" Julius said.

Ethan didn't know if Julius had heard the conversation or not. Ms. Gunderson's voice was always so soft and low.

"She just wanted to ask me about one answer I put down on yesterday's homework," Ethan lied. It was better than telling the truth: *She was just praising me for being a hero.*

But Ethan knew he had deserved only the first part of Ms. Gunderson's praise, not the second. He *wasn't* being particularly kind to Lizzie. He was as deeply involved in the contest scam as anyone. Even more deeply. He was the one who had told her about it in the first place.

Right then, halfway to art class, Ethan made a solemn vow: He would tell Lizzie the truth about the contest. He would tell her today.

During art class, while he was supposed to be sketching a still life of a bowl of bananas, Ethan made himself open Marcia's valentine and Lizzie's note. Marcia's valentine was a regular, elementary-school-type valentine, with a foil-covered chocolate heart stuck to it. Ethan ate the chocolate right away. He needed to keep up his strength.

Then he unfolded the slip of paper Lizzie had left on his desk. Sure enough, it was a poem.

For Ethan

Today is the day we speak our love,
So I will speak my love for you.
It is yours, if you should want
A love that is forever true.

It is yours, if you should want
A love that burns with endless flame,
A love that will outlast the hills,
And all of earthly glory and fame.

At the bottom in tiny print she signed her initials: E.A. Lizzie was short for Elizabeth.

Ethan took a deep breath after he finished reading. It certainly didn't make him look forward to sitting next to its author for Peer-Assisted Learning in another twenty minutes. He made a mental entry in *Life Isn't Fair: A Proof*.

Friday, February 14. Lizzie Archer gave Ethan Winfield a valentine. Lizzie Archer, who cannot

even light a match, loves Ethan Winfield with a
love that burns with endless flame.

Did Lizzie really like him that much? She hardly
knew him. Of course, you could say that he hardly
knew Grace Gunderson, but he liked her that much. He
felt as if his love for her would be forever true. It would
burn with endless flame. It would outlast the hills. And
while, as the vice president of Losers, Inc., Ethan
wasn't expecting much in the way of earthly glory and
fame, whatever he got of it he'd give to her.

Ethan tore a sheet of paper from the back of his
sketchpad. He knew what he was going to do. Sitting
right there in art class, he was going to write Ms. Gunderson a poem.

He had written poems before, for school assignments, but they had all been terrible. How did you go
about writing a *good* poem, a poem that would really
tell another person what you wanted to say?

Ignoring the bowl of bananas, Ethan picked up his
pencil and wrote: "My love for you is like . . ." But he
didn't know how to finish the line. Like what? What *was*
it like?

How did Lizzie do it?

He thought about Grace Gunderson standing in front
of the class that morning, giving the bunsen burner
demonstration, looking beautiful even in safety goggles. But safety goggles weren't poetic enough to put
into a poem.

Suddenly he had an idea. Quickly he wrote: "My love for you is like / A bunsen burner burning bright." Then another line came to him, and another after that. Some of his lines didn't rhyme, but every year teachers told them that poems didn't have to rhyme. Lizzie always managed to get hers to rhyme, though.

When Ethan's poem was done, he read it over one last time. It was actually pretty good—not as good as Lizzie's poems, but definitely the best poem he had ever written. Best of all, it said what he wanted to say.

For Grace Gunderson

My love for you is like
A bunsen burner burning bright.
It burns all day.
It burns all night.
However cold it gets outside
There's a part of me inside
That stays warm.
When it gets dark outside
There's a part of me inside
That is light,
Like a bunsen burner burning bright.

At the bottom he signed it: "Your Secret Admirer." His banana still life ended up looking like a bowl of yellow hot dogs, but he didn't care.

On the way to math class, he stopped in the office and slipped the paper into Ms. Gunderson's mailbox. The Russell Stover and Whitman's candy boxes were gone, but now there was a foil-wrapped Russell Stover chocolate-covered strawberry-cream heart and a small bag of those candy hearts with corny messages on them.

And one poem. No long-stemmed red rose. But one poem.

Ten

As Ethan made himself walk into math class third period, he felt like Sydney Carton from *A Tale of Two Cities* walking to his execution at the guillotine.

It had been bad enough being Lizzie's partner for Peer-Assisted Learning before she had "spoken her love." Then he had known she had a crush on him, but he hadn't *officially* known. As of today, he knew. And he knew that she knew that he knew.

And today was the day that he had made his solemn vow to tell Lizzie about the contest, or be forever unworthy of Grace Gunderson.

As if Ethan weren't already miserable enough, he overheard Julius talking to Barnett and Ryan.

"Do you want to come over on Saturday to help me with my science fair project?" Julius was asking them.

"Nah," Barnett said.

"It has to do with pigging out on ice cream," Julius added.

"Yeah!" Barnett said.

"Count me in," Alex said, gesturing with an imaginary spoon.

Ethan couldn't blame Julius for not inviting him. And yet he did. Were he and Julius best friends or not?

Luckily, Mr. Grotient didn't make them begin Peer-Assisted Learning right away. As he laid out some new, complicated problems on the chalkboard, Ethan had time to consider his situation.

He decided to pretend that he had never read Lizzie's poem. After all, twenty minutes ago he *hadn't* read it. He might not have read it until after school. Or tomorrow morning. Or sometime next week. He might have lost it before he ever had a chance to read it. He would act as if nothing had happened. He'd start in with some question about today's math problems as if February the fourteenth were a day like any other.

Except that, at the same time that he was acting as if nothing had happened, he also had to break the truth to her about the contest. It wouldn't have been as awful if he hadn't been the one who had told her about it in the first place.

Oh, Lizzie? Remember that contest I was talking about last week? The one you said I was so nice to tell you about? Well, it was all part of a mean joke that Barnett and Ryan and Marcia and I were trying to play on you.

How could Ethan say that?

He couldn't.

But he had to.

When it was time for Peer-Assisted Learning, Ethan took the lead in moving his desk. Lizzie's face was scarlet, redder than her hair. It occurred to Ethan that, in addition to the poem, she had the bunsen burner business to blush about, too. Ethan wouldn't have wanted to be Lizzie today.

"So," Ethan said in his best fake, cheerful, nothing-has-happened voice, "did you get any of what Grotient was saying?" *He* certainly didn't.

"A little bit," Lizzie whispered, looking away, her face hidden by her hair.

"Like, on that first problem he did, I didn't really get his explanation of why he was doing it that way."

"Well, I think he was trying to show that it doesn't matter if x is in the numerator or in the denominator. You solve for it in basically the same way in both cases."

Leave it to Lizzie to understand math perfectly even when she was overcome with shame and humiliation. Ethan had to admire her for that. And she had been pretty brave to put her initials on the valentine poem. She hadn't signed *her* poem "A Secret Admirer."

After Lizzie had shown him how to do a few of the new problems, Ethan forced himself to face his confession.

"Um—Lizzie?"

"What?"

He had to say it.

He couldn't say it.

"That contest? The one I told you about? Did you ever enter it?"

"Oh, yes. I sent my poem in right away. I forget when you're supposed to hear. I don't think it said on the announcement. Usually they tell you, but I don't think this one did. Not that I expect to win or anything. I told you before, I've never won a contest. But I love entering them, anyway."

"These contests—do you think—I mean, are they always—like, real?"

Lizzie looked puzzled. "Real? You mean, do they really give you a prize if you win? I guess so. Since I've never won, I don't know much about what happens if you do. But maybe this time I'll find out, right?"

Ethan tried again. "I read somewhere that some contests are phony. Like some lotteries. They get you to buy something, but you don't have any real chance of winning."

"With writing contests you don't have to buy anything," Lizzie said.

And in this case it wasn't that Lizzie had no chance of winning but that she had a one hundred percent chance of winning.

Ethan gave up. "Well, I hope you win," he said. What else could he say?

At least he'd tried to tell her, Ethan told himself defensively. But he knew, as much as he knew anything, that trying wasn't good enough.

"How was school?" Ethan's mother asked at dinner.

"Fine," Peter said.

"Fine," Ethan said, but today the lie was too much for him. "Except that it was Valentine's Day," he added.

His father looked over at him sympathetically. Ethan had never seen his father give his mother a valentine. But it was clear that they loved each other. They showed it in other ways—like looking proud when the other one was dressed up, or holding hands when they took a walk.

"Did you both get some valentines?" his mother asked.

Peter nodded, but didn't volunteer any more information. Ethan knew that a couple of girls at school liked Peter, because they called him all the time. As far as he knew, Peter didn't like any girls, except as friends. He and Peter never talked about things like that.

"What about you, Ethan?"

"I got a couple." And he had given one Valentine's Day poem. He wondered if Ms. Gunderson had read it yet, and, if so, if she had any idea who had sent it. He hoped she wouldn't think it was from Julius. Though Julius didn't look like the type to write poetry. Not that

Ethan was the type to write poetry, either. At least, he hadn't been until today.

"I take it that Valentine's Day is not your favorite holiday?" Ethan's mother patted his hand. "Well, you should have been at Little Wonders this morning. Imagine twenty children, each with nineteen valentines to hand out, in my class alone. That's almost four hundred valentines. None of them can read. Their parents are frantic to get to work. So the teachers are trying to take off jackets, boots, snow pants, hats, and mittens—*while* stuffing four hundred valentines into the flimsy little paper bag mail pouches that I had the bright idea of making. Then the four hundred valentines have to be opened, and read aloud to their recipients, and counted, and crumpled, and lost, and found again, and stuffed back into the bags, which are now beginning to tear."

"What about Edison Blue?" Ethan asked. "Was he there today?"

"Yes." The single syllable had a great deal of misery compressed into it. "He was there. Edison decided he didn't want to give away his valentines. He wanted to keep them all for himself. I wouldn't have made an issue of it, but Edison's mom had obviously spent a lot of time making the valentines and was determined to get them delivered. What a battle *that* was."

"Who won?" Ethan's dad asked.

"Who do you think? That was how most of the mail

pouches got torn—with Edison trying to get every last one of his valentines back. Complicated, of course, by the fact that he had only a vague idea of which ones were his, as one small white envelope looks very much like another. The only good thing I can say about Valentine's Day is that it's a whole year until we get another one."

Ethan's sentiments exactly.

Ethan spent most of Saturday bouncing balls for his science fair project. He wondered if Julius was spending the day eating ice cream with Barnett and Ryan. Ethan tried to ignore his hurt. He needed to stay home and work on his project, anyway, for the fair was only a week and a half away.

Ethan planned to drop ten different balls onto five different surfaces: the wooden floor of the living room, the carpeted floor of the family room, the linoleum floor of the kitchen, the concrete floor of the garage, and the old trampoline he and Peter used to jump on when they were little. On the wall behind every bouncing zone he hung a measuring tape. Then Ethan dropped each ball in turn, and Peter measured the height that it bounced.

"This is a really cool project," Peter said as Ethan began dropping the tennis ball onto the concrete floor of the garage. "Three feet. I wouldn't be surprised if the judges picked it to go to the regional fair. They get sick of the same old stuff. Like mine. Mine is the hundred-thousandth project on electromagnetism. Yours is something really different."

"You'll get picked," Ethan said. "You always get picked." He tried to keep the hint of bitterness out of his voice.

Peter couldn't contradict him. He always *did* get picked. "Three feet one inch. Well, if you want some pointers, neatness counts. Neatness counts a *lot*. The judges go in for the really spiffy displays. Every year I've seen kids with terrific projects not get picked because their displays are a mess. And the judges like it if you act real enthusiastic about your project. I mean, you shouldn't put on an act or anything. But if *you're* enthusiastic about a project, chances are they will be, too."

Ethan dropped his golf ball. It hardly bounced at all.

"Two inches," Peter read off the tape. "How come you and Julius aren't working together this time?"

Ethan shrugged. He dropped the ball again.

"Two and a half inches. I think it's a good idea, going off on your own. Julius is a good kid, but . . ."

Ethan felt his face flushing. Nobody had asked Peter to critique his friends. "But what?"

"It's just that he—you know. He likes being—well, I wouldn't call him a loser, exactly, but he's a . . ."

Loser.

"No, he's not," Ethan said. "He's just not into grades

and things. And impressing people. But he's smarter than he looks. This year he has a great science project, too. He really does. And he's nice." A series of memories flashed through Ethan's mind. Julius defending Ethan against Alex's teasing. Julius defending Ethan against Ms. Leeds's accusations. Julius being the only one not to agree to the prank against Lizzie. "He's the best kid I know."

"Look, don't get mad." Peter handed Ethan the basketball. "I said he was a good kid. I just think you have a better chance at winning the science fair on your own, that's all."

Ethan dropped the basketball.

"Three feet," Peter read out.

Ethan dropped it again.

"Two feet ten inches."

Winning the science fair isn't everything, you know, Ethan wanted to say to Peter. He didn't say it. For the truth was that Ethan wanted to win the science fair. He couldn't remember the last time he had wanted anything as much.

By four-thirty all of Ethan's data had been collected. He and Peter gave each other exuberant high fives. Now if Ethan won the Nobel Prize, in his acceptance speech he'd definitely have to thank Peter along with Grace Gunderson. Peter had helped him for four solid hours, even though his own project still wasn't finished. It was more than a lot of brothers would have done.

"Hey, I have an idea," Peter said. "Let's go outside and bounce some basketballs."

Ethan laughed. "I'm going to dream about bouncing balls tonight."

"What about dinner?"

Satisfaction in the afternoon's work made Ethan feel ready for anything. He had a sudden urge to make something fancy. Like crepes Suzette. Whatever they were. Or something on fire. Though, on second thought, the bunsen burners had been enough fire for one week. Maybe a cake like the ones he liked to look at in the window of the French bakery in the shopping center.

"Let's bake a cake," he said.

"A cake?" Peter sounded surprised. The boys almost never made desserts. The most ambitious desserts they had ever attempted were Betty Crocker brownies and instant chocolate pudding.

"Yeah. For the dinner part, we can just have scrambled eggs or something. But for dessert, let's make a cake." In his mind Ethan already had a name for the cake, though he'd never tell it to Peter.

La Grace.

Peter found an easy-looking recipe in one of the cookbooks on the kitchen shelf. Ethan gathered all the ingredients.

But the cake was a failure. For starters, the layers wouldn't come out of the pans. Ethan turned the pans over onto the cake racks, burning his hand on one of them, and then pounded the bottoms again and again.

"You're not doing it right," Peter said. He took over, whacking the pans until he dented the metal. The cakes still wouldn't come out.

"Maybe there's something wrong with the pans," Peter suggested.

"They're the same ones Mom uses all the time," Ethan couldn't resist pointing out.

Finally, the top half came out of one pan, but the bottom half stayed in, stuck to the pan as firmly as if they had glued it there with household cement. And when Ethan ate a chunk of the part that was stuck in the pan, it had a funny, rubbery texture. Ethan was sure that if they dropped the cake into a sink full of water, it wouldn't fall apart; it would just sink to the bottom, and then they'd be able to wring it out and put it back on the plate.

"I think we forgot to put something in," Ethan said.

"Yeah," Peter agreed ruefully. "Like whatever the stuff is that gives cakes their flavor."

Their parents came home from shopping as Ethan was scraping both pans of La Grace into the trash. He hoped the cake wasn't an omen. He shouldn't have called it La Grace. He should have called it La Lizzie.

But he felt oddly cheerful that he and Peter shared the blame for its failure.

"Something smells . . ."

Ethan could tell that his mother had planned to say good, but at the last minute changed her mind.

"Terrible?" Peter asked.

"Interesting," she said.

"It was a cake," Peter told her. "It was interesting, all right. I hope I don't make anything that interesting again for a long time. Scrambled eggs, anyone?"

"Let's get a pizza," their dad said, coming to the rescue.

At dinner, Peter didn't need much coaxing to tell their parents about the work they had done all afternoon on Ethan's science fair project. "It's looking great," he said.

"It certainly sounds it," Ethan's mother said. "I have a feeling that this is the year we're going to have two Winfield projects chosen for the regional science fair!"

Ethan wished she hadn't said it. She always tried too hard to act as if he were as successful as Peter. And he wasn't. He had never had a project chosen for the regional science fair. Peter had never had a project that wasn't chosen.

But maybe this year would be different. Peter honestly seemed to think that the sports project was good. So did Grace Gunderson. Of course, Julius had said she thought his ice cream project was great, too.

Maybe *both* their projects would be picked for the regional science fair: Three projects could be chosen from each grade. That would really be something for Losers, Inc. Maybe it was time to start drafting that Nobel acceptance speech, after all.

Eleven

On Monday morning Ethan awoke with a vague sense of uneasiness. But he couldn't think of anything to be uneasy about. He had survived Valentine's Day. He had collected all the data for his science project. Julius had come over on Sunday, and they had watched a really funny Pink Panther video. It had almost seemed like old times.

So why should Ethan feel weighed down with worry? He was obviously forgetting something important—and terrible. But what?

He was halfway to school before he remembered.

The valentine poem.

He had taken care not to sign his name, but he had forgotten to disguise his handwriting. Ethan had very distinctive handwriting—square and blocky, almost like printing. If Ms. Gunderson had the slightest bit of curiosity about the poem, she'd be able to figure out who had written it from the handwriting alone. She already knew that he and Julius had searched out her apartment the other day. Now she would know that he was the author of the bunsen-burner poem as well.

Was that so terrible?

Yes.

Ethan didn't want Ms. Gunderson to think of him the way he thought of Lizzie. He wanted her to think of him as a promising young scientist, not a promising young lovesick, poetry-writing scientist.

In science class first period, she seemed the same as always, though when she spoke to Ethan her voice sounded even more gentle. But perhaps that was because she was using it to make a special request.

"Boys and girls, we're going to be working at the lab tables again today. Marcia, would you and Julius be partners? And, Ethan, why don't you be partners with Lizzie?"

Great. Now he was Lizzie's partner in math *and* science. Ethan knew why Ms. Gunderson had reassigned the lab partners: She didn't want Marcia spending the whole class period teasing Lizzie about not being able to light a bunsen burner. Once again she had cast Ethan in the hero role, so once again he had no choice but to be a hero.

At the lab table, he lit the burner for the two of them, sort of like the lead in an old movie lighting a cigarette to hand to the woman he loved. Only Ethan was lighting it for Grace and handing it to Lizzie. So to speak.

The others teased Lizzie anyway.

"Spazzie? I mean, Lizzie? Can we borrow your matches?" That was Alex, from the table next to them. "Unless you're afraid to touch the matchbox."

Ethan handed Alex the matchbox in silence, without dignifying Alex's remark with a reply. He sometimes wondered why some people were so mean. He had met Alex's dad a couple of times, and Mr. Ryan was mean, too. So maybe Alex thought that was how you had to act to be a guy.

As the bell rang, Ms. Gunderson again asked Ethan to stay for a minute. Private after-class chats with her were becoming routine.

"Ethan, I hope you don't mind that I asked you to work with Lizzie."

Ethan shook his head. He tried to strike a gallant pose.

"I think you have a lot to offer Lizzie. And she might have something to offer you, too."

Like endless love until her doom, Ethan thought glumly, but he kept the gallant, heroic look on his face.

"Lizzie is such a talented poet . . . You write poetry, too, don't you, Ethan?"

Ethan shook his head again, more emphatically than before, but he felt the color rising in his face, and he couldn't meet Ms. Gunderson's eyes.

"Well, anyway, thank you, Ethan."

She bent to straighten the papers on her desk. Ethan didn't know if she was thanking him for helping Lizzie. Or for his poem. Or both. But he felt a rush of grateful relief as he turned to go.

Then another, even more terrible thought struck him. Two more weeks. That was all the time Ms. Gunderson had left at West Creek Middle School. Two more weeks.

At lunch on Wednesday, Marcia sat down next to Ethan and Julius.

"Ta-dah!" she said, producing a piece of paper from her immaculately neat notebook.

Ethan's heart sank. Was it another love poem stolen from Lizzie? But what Marcia had was even worse.

"I wrote the letter."

Ethan must have looked blank.

"The *letter*. To the Lizard. Telling her she won first prize in the contest. Do you want to hear it?"

Neither Ethan nor Julius replied. Marcia began to read:

Dear Miss Archer:

We are pleased to tell you that your poem "Snow Bird" has won first prize in the entire nation out of all the entries in the National Poetry Contest.

The judges were particularly impressed by its

lovely imagery. You are a young poet of extraordinary talent.

Congratulations on winning this prestigious award.

Sincerely,

Mr. Archibald Q. Smith

"Did you like the part about the lovely imagery?" Marcia asked. "I don't know what lovely imagery is exactly, but I thought it sounded good. I thought the name Archibald Q. Smith sounded good, too."

"Did you mail it to her?" Ethan asked.

"Of course not, silly. I mailed it to my cousin, and *she'll* mail it to Lizzie. So that it has a Washington, D.C., postmark. So what do you think? Does it sound okay?"

It would have sounded okay if it had been a real contest instead of a cruel hoax. Ethan knew that Julius was waiting to hear what he said next. "I don't know," he said slowly. "I don't think we should tell Lizzie that she won the contest."

"You think we should tell her that she *lost* the contest?" Marcia asked. "Would that be better?"

Ethan didn't know. Were you more of a failure if you lost a fake contest or if you won it?

He tried again. "I don't think we should tell her anything. It's like, the joke has gone far enough. I think you should call your cousin and tell her we changed our minds."

"Ethan," Marcia said in a mock-scolding tone, "have you changed *your* mind? Are you chickening out?"

Before Ethan could answer, Marcia went on, "Look, I already mailed the letter to my cousin. I'm not calling her again. My mom makes me pay for my own long-distance calls, you know. It's just a *joke*. Lizzie should be able to take one little joke."

Marcia flounced away from the table. Julius didn't say anything, but Ethan knew that Julius thought he had failed Lizzie once again.

Over the weekend Peter helped Ethan put all the data for his science fair project into a spreadsheet on the computer. It took a long time, but when everything was printed out, his tables and graphs looked fantastic. How could the judges not be blown away by tables and graphs like these? They looked as if they had been made by a real scientist—a real, Nobel Prize–winning scientist—not by a twelve-year-old kid who, until a month ago, hadn't even been good at science.

Peter's graphs looked like Nobel Prize winners, too. But that was okay. Ethan and Peter weren't competing against each other. The judges would choose three projects from each grade. Sixth graders competed against other sixth graders, and eighth graders competed against other eighth graders.

But Ethan was competing against *Julius*, in a sense.

Though both of their projects could end up being picked as two out of the three sixth-grade winners. It would certainly be wild if they were.

On Sunday, after lunch, Julius called Ethan.

"You want to come over and eat some ice cream?" he asked.

Ethan's mood soared, but he kept his voice casual. "Sure."

At Julius's house, Julius was all business as he led Ethan to a kitchen chair, then blindfolded him.

"In case fat-free ice cream looks different," Julius explained. "I have three flavors for people to taste, with regular and fat-free versions of each. Guess which three flavors? No, don't guess. Vanilla, chocolate, and strawberry. Original, huh? Okay, vanilla first. Open wide! Round and round the airplane goes, and *in*to the airport!"

Julius fed Ethan the first spoonful. It tasted pretty good. All ice cream tasted pretty good to Ethan. Then Julius fed him the second spoonful. It tasted a lot better—richer, creamier . . . fatter.

"Which tasted better?" Julius asked.

"The second one."

Ethan tasted the chocolate and the strawberry. The second one tasted better each time. Then Julius removed the blindfold.

"And the winner is—the real stuff! Dripping and oozing with saturated fat!"

Ethan laughed. "This *is* a cool project," he said. He didn't know whether he should stop there or not. "I bet it gets picked for the regional science fair. I hope it does."

Julius began rinsing off Ethan's spoons, six of them, one for each taste. Ethan could tell that he had said the wrong thing, but he didn't see why. He *did* hope Julius's ice cream project would be picked as a winner. He just hoped even more that his own ball-bouncing project would win.

The day before the science fair, a heavy snow came in from the plains, but snow almost never closed school in West Creek. Since it was too snowy for the boys to ride their bikes, Ethan's father dropped Ethan and Peter at school on his way to work.

It was snowing so hard that Ethan could hardly see out the windows in science class. Lizzie sat beside him at their lab table, staring dreamily out at the storm, probably groping for words for another poem. The flakes definitely didn't look like floating wisps of cotton today. The snow looked more like—Ethan couldn't think of a good way to describe it.

"A white fury—raving—blind," Lizzie said, as if to herself.

Yes, that was what it looked like, all right.

Ethan wondered if Lizzie had gotten the letter yet about "Snow Bird." It should be coming in the mail any day now. But he made himself focus on the science experiment instead.

They were starting distillation of wood. As usual, Ethan lit the bunsen burner. The snowstorm raging outside made the classroom seem bright and safe, almost cozy.

As Alex lit his burner at the table next to them, he waved his match toward Lizzie. "Fire!" he cackled, in what was plainly intended to be a Wicked Witch of the West voice. "This is what I have for you, my little ugly! Fire!"

Lizzie flinched, but she didn't scream. Ethan was relieved.

"Here, Spazzie, catch!"

Alex blew out the match first, then tossed it, still smoking, directly in front of Lizzie on their lab table. This time Lizzie did scream.

Ms. Gunderson hurried over. "What happened? Lizzie?"

Lizzie didn't answer, but Alex's self-satisfied smirk gave him away.

"Alex, you will leave Lizzie alone, or you will spend the rest of this class period in the office. Do you understand?"

Alex's smirk disappeared. Ms. Gunderson so seldom yelled at anyone that it was impressive when she did. But as soon as she turned to go to another table, Alex hissed at them, "Nice scream, Spazzie."

That was when Ethan decided: He was going to teach Lizzie how to light a bunsen burner.

When the bell rang for the end of class, Ethan leaned over to Lizzie. "Lizzie, wait. Look, you're going to have to learn how to light this thing, or else Alex and those guys are going to keep teasing you. It's easy. It really is. I'll show you. It'll just take a minute."

Lizzie shook her head, but she didn't get up to go.

"All you have to do, if the match starts to burn your finger, is blow it out. Like a birthday candle. You've blown out birthday candles, right?"

Lizzie nodded.

"Okay. Here's a match. Go ahead, light it."

"I can't."

"Sure you can. Come on. Just light it."

Lizzie struck the match. It lit. Her hand trembled, but she didn't drop the match and she didn't scream.

"Okay. Turn on the gas. With your other hand. Turn on the gas."

Lizzie did it.

"Now blow out the match. Good. Now turn off the gas."

Lizzie obeyed.

"You did it! You lit the bunsen burner! Okay, do it again. Here's another match. Light it."

Lizzie lit the bunsen burner again.

The second-period kids were coming in now, but Ethan held out one last match to Lizzie. "One more time."

Lizzie lit it again.

Ethan looked at Ms. Gunderson. She was watching them with a grateful smile. For once he had earned that smile. He could die right now, having done one thing in his life to truly earn her praise.

Twelve

On the morning of the science fair, Ethan's father loaded both boys' project displays into the back of his van, as Ethan hunted frantically on the floor of his closet for a tie. He definitely owned at least one tie: He wore it to church every year on Easter Sunday. But last Easter was almost a year ago, and Ethan hadn't seen his tie since.

He hated having to ask his mom to find it, but his dad was already in the van, honking his horn. "Mom! Have you seen my tie anywhere?"

Ethan's mother didn't show any expression on her face as she took the tie off the hook at the rear of his closet and handed it to him. But once he had managed to remember how to tie it, she gave him a hug. "I can't help it," she said. "You and Peter both look so handsome today. I'm so proud of both of you."

The tie had been Peter's idea. "That's another

thing," he had told Ethan the night before. "Personal appearance. The judges love it if you comb your hair and shine your shoes and wear a tie."

Ethan hadn't shined his shoes; he still wore his old high-tops. But he had jerked a comb through his hair. And he had to admit that he looked pretty sharp in his tie. The guys Ms. Gunderson hung out with at the university probably wore ties all the time. Quickly Ethan drove the thought away.

At school, Ethan's dad helped them carry their displays into the gym. "Good luck, boys," he said gruffly and then hurried off to his first carpet-cleaning job of the morning.

Ethan swallowed hard. He had entered the science fair every year, but this was the first year he had cared about winning. It was embarrassing having his parents see that he cared. And between his carefully constructed display and neatly knotted tie, this year everybody at school was going to know that he cared. Ethan thought about taking off his tie and putting it back on after lunch, when the fair would be open for judging. He decided to keep it on, at least through science class.

But when Julius saw him in homeroom, Julius looked so betrayed that Ethan turned away. *Losers don't wear ties.* Julius hadn't said it out loud, but he might as well have.

Ms. Gunderson was dressed up, too, in a new blue

dress that had kind of an olden-days look to it. She looked nervous herself as she greeted the class at the start of first period.

"Today is our big day," she said. "I know all of you have worked very hard. You have produced some truly outstanding projects."

Ethan flushed. He felt as if Ms. Gunderson were talking directly to him. Though maybe Julius thought she was talking directly to *him*.

"I hope that some of you will have the satisfaction of having your projects chosen to go on to the regional science fair. As you know, three projects will be chosen for each grade. But, more important, I hope that your participation in this year's science fair has taught you something about the excitement of conducting your own scientific research."

Ms. Gunderson brushed back a strand of hair that had escaped from the rest. "This is our last week together," she said softly.

Ethan's heart tightened, as if Ms. Gunderson had clamped a vise around it. He had known from the start that she was going to be at West Creek Middle School for only five weeks, but he couldn't believe that the time had passed so quickly. He couldn't imagine what school—or life—would be like without her.

"I just want to say that I'm enormously impressed by what you have achieved in the past few weeks. Today is a remarkable day. I'm never going to forget it."

For a moment Ethan was afraid that she was going

to cry. Then she smiled at them. "Let's go," she said.

She led the class to the gym, to practice the presentations they were going to give the judges that afternoon.

"Who wants to go first?" she asked, once they were all assembled by the sixth-grade displays.

Ethan's hand shot up in the air.

"Ethan?"

Ethan had written out his speech and practiced it at home in front of his bedroom mirror. It came out sounding almost as memorized as one of Lizzie's book reports. He explained his procedure and gave each of the ten balls a demonstration bounce on the small wooden platform his father had helped him build for his display. Then he pointed to the graphs of his data that Peter had helped him make on the computer.

"Oh, Ethan!" Ms. Gunderson said when he had finished. The other kids crowded up with questions.

"Hey, let me try bouncing a couple of your balls," someone said. It was Alex Ryan, for a change sounding not mean but honestly interested. Lizzie's eyes were shining. Ethan could imagine the poem about him that she was composing in her head.

Only Julius held back, staring down sullenly at the gymnasium floor. But from everything Ethan had seen of it, Julius's project was just as good as Ethan's. Julius had no reason to be jealous or resentful of what his friend had achieved.

"All right," Ms. Gunderson said. "We have so many

wonderful projects to admire that we'd better move on. Alex and David, what do you have for us?"

They had done the same project some kid did every year, the one where you mix baking soda with vinegar to make a gas that blows up a balloon. Their display looked pretty nice, though, with color photos of how the balloon looked when it was blown up and all the explanations of everything typed up on David's computer.

Then it was Lizzie's turn. Her project was called "The Sources of Poetic Imagination." She had done just as Ethan had suggested. She had written to twenty poets to ask how they got the ideas for their poems; fourteen had written back, and Lizzie had their letters displayed attractively on her poster board, together with a sample poem from each poet. It had turned out to be a pretty decent project, after all, but Ethan didn't think she had a real chance of winning the science fair. It was still an English project, not a science project, whatever Ms. Gunderson said about how everything and anything could count as science.

Lizzie had included herself as the fifteenth poet in her display. Ethan gave a quick glance toward the poster board to see which poem she had chosen. It was "Snow Bird," the same poem that she had sent in to the fake contest.

"Very nice, Lizzie!" Ms. Gunderson said. "One of these days, when your poems are published, we're all going to remember this moment and say, 'We knew her when.' "

"Actually," Lizzie said, and stopped. "Well, I don't want to brag, but I'm just so *excited* that I have to tell *somebody*. My poem? The one on the display? It just won a prize. In a contest. For the whole country. The letter came yesterday."

Behind Ethan, Marcia giggled. Ethan didn't think Lizzie heard her. He felt choked, suffocated, as if his tie were strangling him. He had been too much of a coward to tell her, too much of a coward to stop the others, and now it was too late.

"Congratulations!" Ms. Gunderson said. "That is splendid news, Lizzie! All right, who's next? Marcia, what do you and Susan have for us?"

Half a dozen other groups presented their projects —none of them as good as Ethan's, in his honest opinion—and then Ms. Gunderson turned to Julius.

"Julius?"

Ethan gave Julius an encouraging smile. This should be as proud a moment for Julius as it had been for him, for everybody else. But Julius looked anything but proud. And as soon as Ethan looked at Julius's display, he could see why.

As Peter would have said, Julius's display was a mess. He could have had a great project. It was certainly more original than Alex and David's, less strange than Lizzie's. And everybody loved ice cream. But Julius should have arranged his data into a graph. He should have typed his labels on the computer. He should have had somebody take photographs of one of the tasting sessions. He should have done *something* that showed some effort.

"Regular ice cream or fat-free ice cream: Which tastes better?" Julius read from an index card in the flat, monotonous voice he used for book reports. "My hypothesis was: Regular ice cream tastes better. Ten people tasted my samples. They all said that regular ice cream tastes better. So regular ice cream tastes better." Then he put his card away.

"Did you bring any ice cream for people to taste at the science fair?" David asked.

"No," Julius said, grinning for the first time that morning. Ethan felt better.

"The way Ethan brought balls for us to bounce?"

Julius's grin disappeared. Ethan felt worse.

"Do we have anyone left?" Ms. Gunderson asked. "No? Then let's go back to class. Good luck this afternoon, everyone!"

All afternoon classes were canceled for the science fair. Hundreds of students and dozens of teachers filled the gym, plus any parents who didn't have to work that day—and the judges.

Ethan's display attracted more attention than any of the other sixth-grade displays nearby. Over and over again he bounced his demonstration balls and explained his results. His was definitely the most popular display with the students. And several of his teachers lingered, too. Even Mr. Grotient took a turn bouncing the basketball. He looked a bit like a basketball himself, with a black-and-white bow tie painted on one side.

"By the way, Ethan," he said in a low voice as he handed the ball back to Ethan, "I'm in the process of grading last week's math tests, and I must say you did very well."

Ethan was surprised, but not very surprised. The test had been the easiest one Mr. Grotient had given all year.

"That test was my toughest yet," Mr. Grotient said, straightening his bow tie, which didn't need straightening. "I think we have Peer-Assisted Learning to thank for this, don't you?"

The Lizard! Well, that could be. Ethan usually understood a problem better after Lizzie explained it. If only he hadn't agreed to go along with the contest scam. If only he hadn't been the one who had told her to apply. If only the contest were a real one that she had really won.

"May I have a turn?" someone else asked. Ethan turned off his guilty thoughts about Lizzie. And Julius.

The judges finally came to Ethan's display around two-thirty—a man and a woman, each carrying a clipboard. By now Ethan had explained his project so many times to so many people that any trace of nervousness was gone. He looked them in the eyes as he answered their questions, the way Peter had told him to do. When they were done, he thanked them and shook their hands. He felt as if he *were* Peter, making a successful, game-saving free throw in front of a gym packed with cheering fans. Maybe he *would* be a scientist someday.

The judges moved on to Marcia's display. Julius would be next.

With the judges' visit behind him, Ethan could leave his booth now and walk around for a bit. He acted as if he were just strolling aimlessly about, but he stopped by Julius's display.

"Hi," Ethan said.

"Hi," Julius said.

Ethan looked again at Julius's almost bare rectangle of poster board, with its crooked lettering squeezed too close to the top. It wasn't fair that Ethan had had so much help from Peter, while Julius hadn't gotten any help from anybody. Maybe Ethan should have worked with Julius, after all. Ethan wished that Julius could be sharing his moment of triumph instead of standing alone—hurt, jealous, abandoned.

"When the judges come?" Ethan said awkwardly. "Well, Peter told me—it's a good idea to look them in the eye when you talk to them. And thank them when they're done. And, you know, shake their hands."

Julius didn't say anything. But he didn't look particularly grateful for Ethan's suggestions.

Ethan tried again. "It's just that—they like enthusi-asm, Peter said. They like it if you act enthusiastic."

"What if you're not?" Julius asked. His voice was so hard and cold that Ethan took a step backward, as if Julius had hit him. "Maybe I'm not as good as you are at pretending to be something I'm not."

"It's not pretending, not really," Ethan said. He found himself becoming angry at Julius. It wasn't pre-tending to try to do your best at something—though Ethan had the sudden, uncomfortable thought that he *had* been pretending to be nice to Lizzie, to be the kind, concerned friend Ms. Gunderson thought him to be. But as for the rest, he wasn't *pretending*: He was really, genuinely trying to do his best.

It was Julius's own fault that he was such a loser. He didn't have to be. At least he could have printed the title of his project *neatly*. How hard would it have been to do that?

"You don't *have* to be a loser, you know," Ethan blurted out. "It's like you *try* to be a loser."

"Well, you don't have to be *friends* with a loser," Julius shot back. He was shouting now, the way he had shouted at Ms. Leeds on the day of the book reports. That day he had been taking Ethan's side, as Ethan's best friend. Now the friendship was over.

"Excuse me, boys."

The judges had arrived at Julius's display. Ethan turned and walked away.

Thirteen

As he rode his bike home from school on the snowy streets, alone, Ethan's thoughts bounced back and forth, as if some crazy Ping-Pong game were playing itself out in his head.

Ping! He had had the best science fair project in the first-period class.

Pong! He had had a terrible fight with his best friend and probably would never be friends with him again.

Ping! He heard Grace Gunderson's voice saying, "Oh, Ethan!" after he finished his practice presentation.

Pong! He heard Lizzie's voice saying, "My poem? The one on the display? It just won a prize."

At home, he watched some Looney Tunes on TV to try to settle down, but after a few commercials he turned them off and just lay on the family-room couch, staring at the ceiling.

Would he win the science fair? The judges had definitely acted impressed by his project, but not as impressed as Ms. Gunderson or his classmates. Maybe the judges tried hard *not* to act too impressed.

What if Ethan won for the sixth grade and Peter didn't win for the eighth grade? After leaving Julius, Ethan had walked over to Peter's booth in the eighth-grade section. Peter's display had been perfect, and his experiment was so brilliant and complicated that Ethan couldn't understand half of it. But Ethan had noticed that nobody was hanging around Peter's booth the way kids had been hanging around his. Maybe the judges didn't care whether your project had crowd appeal—but maybe they did. Ethan's victory would be hollow if he couldn't share it with Peter. He wished he were sharing it with Julius.

He even wished he could share it with Lizzie. Lizzie. What would it be like to think you had won a contest and your dream had at last come true, and then find out that your victory—and the whole contest—was just a mean joke?

At dinner, Ethan's mother said, "So tell me all about the science fair! I want to hear every detail!"

"It was all right," Ethan said. The answer wasn't very detailed, so he added, "The kids seemed to like my thing pretty well."

"I'll say!" Peter took a big swig of milk to wash down a mouthful of meat loaf. "It was a mob scene over there."

"What about the judges? Do you think they liked it?" Ethan's mother asked. Then, as if she was afraid she was putting too much pressure on Ethan to win, she said, "It's wonderful that you could get the other kids interested like that. That speaks very well of your experiment. Wouldn't you say so, honey?"

Ethan's father nodded.

"I've forgotten—Peter, last year, how did they let you know you'd won?"

"They called me."

"When?"

"That evening. Like, at eight o'clock. Something like that."

All the Winfields looked at the large clock hung on the kitchen wall. It said seven-fifteen.

"Guess what?" Ethan's mother said then, too heartily. "Guess who had a good day at school today? Edison Blue. We always go outside after snack to play. Everyone except Edison. For the last two weeks or so, he's been on strike. He simply refuses to go outside. I guess one of us could stuff him into his jacket and carry him out bodily, and try not to listen to his screams, but I decided not to force it. So every day, after snack, I offer Edison the chance to go outside, and every day he shouts, 'No!' and then while the rest of us play, he stands by the door, watching us until we come inside again."

Ethan tried not to listen to the ticking of the clock. He had never noticed before how loudly it ticked.

"So today I asked Edison if he wanted to go outside with the rest of us, and he shouted 'No!' the way he always does, and I got the others ready, and we were heading outside when I heard this tremendous sob. I turned around, and it was coming from Edison. 'You never let me go outside!' he was wailing. 'Why, Edison,' I said, 'do you *want* to go outside?' 'Uh-huh,' he said, in this little, wounded, pathetic voice. And he put on his own jacket, and his own hat, and his own mittens, and ran outside and played happily for the rest of the afternoon."

Peter gave a thumb's-up sign as the story ended. Ethan reached over and gave his mother a high five.

The phone rang.

No one got up from the table.

On the second ring, Ethan's mother said, "I'll get it." She picked up the receiver. "Hello? . . . *Oh!* . . . Yes, he's right here." Her voice had become suddenly gentle, and she didn't look at Ethan as she said, "Peter, honey, it's for you."

It could have been that same girl from school, Ashley somebody, who called Peter all the time, but Ethan knew it wasn't. He knew it was the judges, calling to say that Peter had won the science fair. Peter had won, and Ethan hadn't. It was the story of Ethan's life.

Ethan wanted to get up and leave the room, but he

stayed in his seat, listening to Peter's end of the conversation.

"Yes . . . Thank you . . . Thank you . . . I know . . . Yes, he is . . . I'll tell him that . . . Good night."

Peter hung up. He turned toward the table. "I won," he said. His voice was flat. "Ethan, the judges asked me if you were my brother. They said they were very impressed by your energy and enthusiasm and by the originality of your project."

But not impressed enough for you to win.

There was an awkward silence, and then Ethan's mother said, "Oh, Peter, we're thrilled for you. And, Ethan, the judges wouldn't have said that to Peter if they didn't mean it. Peter, tell us again what the judges said about Ethan."

When Peter didn't say anything, their mother hurried on. "Energy *and* enthusiasm *and* originality. Boys, we're so proud of both of you. This calls for a celebration. What can we do to celebrate?"

Peter said, "We don't need to celebrate. Really. It's not that big a deal."

"Of course it is," his mother said.

"I said it isn't. I don't want to."

Ethan knew that Peter was saying it for him. Why did Ethan have to have a brother who was the best in the school at everything—and was a wonderful brother, too? Peter had just won the science fair for the millionth year in a row, but they were all acting as if they were at a funeral. Peter's strained face, his mother's fake cheerfulness, his father's pitying eyes were more than Ethan could bear.

"Stop it!" Ethan suddenly shouted. "Just stop it! All of you!"

He got up so quickly from the table that his chair tipped over. He stooped down to pick it up as the rest of them watched him in silence.

"It's not Peter's *fault* that he won," Ethan said, struggling to get his voice back under control. "And you don't have to go on and on all the time about how wonderful we *both* are. It's like, why do you have to compare people all the time? Peter's Peter, and I'm me. I had fun doing my project, whether it won or not. And *I* know it was good. So I think we *should* have the party."

Peter didn't say anything. Ethan knew he didn't want a party, not when it wasn't for his brother, too.

"Come *on*." Ethan felt as if he was begging Peter.

"Okay," Peter finally said, in a voice Ethan could hardly hear.

"Ethan, I didn't mean—I never meant—" his mother started to say.

"I know," Ethan said, cutting her off. "It's okay. Hey, how about pizza Saturday night, with everything on it —shoot the works."

"Pizza it is," his dad said. His mother, with tears in her eyes, turned away.

Peter didn't say anything more until they were heading up the stairs together to their rooms.

"For what it's worth," he said, turning back to look at Ethan, "you *did* have a good project. You had a *great* project."

Ethan thought back to the afternoon he and Peter had spent bouncing the balls, to Ms. Gunderson's praise that morning, to the crowds of kids hanging around his exhibit all afternoon.

"It *was* great," he said. "I hope I can think of something as terrific as that for next year."

At school the next morning, Ethan stood alone, watching Alex and David and some of the other guys shoot baskets. Twenty feet from him, Julius stood alone, watching them, too. Across the blacktop, Lizzie sat alone, scribbling in her notebook. They formed three points of a triangle, a triangle of losers.

Right that minute, though, Lizzie didn't look like a loser. A small smile played about her mouth. She gazed up thoughtfully at the gray, gloomy sky as if searching for poetic inspiration in the low, snow-threatening clouds. Maybe she was thinking about her next award-winning poem. Had she gone out last night with her parents to celebrate her first prize in the National Poetry Writing Contest?

Ethan couldn't stand it. Whatever else he did in his life, he had to do something about the contest, if it wasn't already too late. He caught David's eye and formed his hands into a T. David tossed the basketball to another kid and came over to where Ethan was standing.

"What's up?"

"This contest thing," Ethan said before he could change his mind. "You guys haven't told Lizzie about it yet, have you? I mean, that it's all fake?"

David shook his head. "She just got the prize letter two days ago."

"I've been thinking," Ethan said desperately. "I don't think we should tell her." He had wanted to tell her before, so she wouldn't fall for the joke, but now that she *had* fallen for it, he couldn't bear the thought of her disappointment.

"It's like, why not let her go on thinking she won something? At this point, telling her—it's too mean."

Ethan had expected David to look disgusted, but he looked almost relieved. "Yeah. I was thinking kind of the same thing. But don't we have to tell her? I mean, she's going to find out, anyway, sooner or later. Some teacher or somebody will try to look the contest up and find out that it doesn't exist."

Ethan scanned the blacktop. He saw Marcia talking to Alex by the bike racks and waved them over. Then he made himself repeat his speech. It came out easier the second time, but right away he could tell that it wasn't going to work as well on these two as it had on David.

"You *do* like Lizzie," Marcia said, her eyes sparkling

with satisfaction. Ethan could practically see her plotting how best to use this knowledge to her own advantage.

No I don't, Ethan was about to say automatically. But it was too much of a lie. It wasn't that he was in love with Lizzie, the way she was with him, the way he was with Ms. Gunderson. But he *did* like her. She was smart. She was more talented than all the rest of them put together. She was even pretty, in her own odd kind of way.

Ethan took a deep breath. "What if I do?" Anyway, whether or not he liked Lizzie wasn't the issue right now. "Telling her—it's just too mean, that's all."

"We wouldn't want to be mean to Ethan's *girl*friend, would we?" Alex asked.

"Look," Marcia said, as if patiently explaining a simple fact to a small child. "We have to tell her. It'd be meaner not to, in a way. We can't let her think it's for real. She's *not* a great poet. She might as well face the truth. Somebody has to help her face it."

The tone of false concern for Lizzie in Marcia's voice made Ethan sick. "You're really going to tell her?" he demanded.

"Somebody has to," Marcia said.

Ethan took a deep breath. "Then I'm going to do it."

"When?" Marcia sounded alarmed.

"Now."

The others watched in silence as Ethan slowly

walked over to where Lizzie was sitting, her notebook still open in her lap. He sat down on the curb next to her.

"Lizzie?"

She smiled up at him.

He plunged on. "The contest you won? The poetry contest? There isn't any. It was all a fake. Alex and David and Marcia . . ." He hesitated. But if he was telling the truth, he was telling the whole truth. "And I— we thought it up as a trick to play on you. I'm sorry. I'm really sorry. I know you probably hate me now, and you should hate me. I hate myself. All I can say is, I'm sorry."

Lizzie stared at him as if she didn't understand what he was saying. Then she hid her face in her hands and began to cry. What was Ethan supposed to do now? He reached out awkwardly and put his hand on her arm. She shook it off and went on crying.

Ethan looked away, wanting to look anywhere but at Lizzie. Suddenly he saw Grace Gunderson, standing across the blacktop as she had that first day, watching the two of them. She couldn't have overheard their conversation, but she could see that Lizzie was crying, and that Ethan was the one who had made her cry. So now she knew. Ethan wasn't a scientist or a hero. He hadn't won the science fair. He was just another mean sixth grader who had broken Lizzie Archer's heart.

Fourteen

Ms. Romero read the names of all the science fair winners during morning announcements. Peter's name was first. Ethan didn't know any of the sixth-grade winners; he felt foolish for ever having dreamed he could be one of them. Ms. Romero also announced that report cards would be handed out at the end of the day. Great.

Lizzie didn't speak to Ethan during science class. At least she lit the bunsen burner for the day's experiment, as calmly as if she had been lighting bunsen burners all her life. Nobody called her Spazzie. But Ethan's triumph over the bunsen burner was empty now.

He wanted to talk to Ms. Gunderson after class, to try to explain to her why Lizzie had been crying, but she was deep in conversation with Mr. O'Keefe. And, besides, what was there to say? The truth was as awful as anything that Ms. Gunderson could be imagining. And this was Ms. Gunderson's last day at West Creek Middle School. Whatever she thought about Ethan now she would think about him forever.

Even in math class, during Peer-Assisted Learning, Lizzie didn't speak to Ethan. Julius wouldn't speak to him at lunch. Ethan had never known that simple silence could make someone so miserable.

In English class, Ms. Leeds assigned another book report. Then she said, with her usual big smile, "Boys and girls, I want to share some exciting news with you. Lizzie told me after class yesterday that one of her poems, 'Snow Bird,' has won first prize in a national writing contest!"

Ms. Leeds led the class in applause. Ethan sat frozen. If he could take back only one minute in his life, it would be the minute when he had agreed to go along with the contest scheme. Or maybe the minute when he had told Lizzie about it.

He looked at Lizzie. She wasn't crying, but there was something in her face that was more terrible than tears.

"*And*," Ms. Leeds went on, not seeming to notice Lizzie's reaction to the first announcement, "I just found out that this same poem has won *another* prize. When Lizzie gave it to me last month, I nominated it for a poetry prize sponsored by the Young Readers Forum, and I got a letter in the mail today saying that it was one of only four poems in the state to be selected for publication."

At first Lizzie's face didn't change. Then Ethan saw a wild hope come into her eyes as she gradually let herself believe that it was true.

Ms. Leeds led the class in a second round of applause. This time, Ethan clapped louder than anyone. He saw that David was clapping, too. Only Alex and Marcia weren't clapping. So Lizzie had the last laugh. Her poems *were* good enough to be published and win a prize.

Ethan waited for Lizzie after class. He didn't think she would listen to him, and he wouldn't blame her if she didn't. But he was going to try to make things right with her, anyway.

"Hey, Lizzie." She stopped walking. "I just wanted to say that I think it's really great, about your prize and all. I really do. And I really truly am sorry about—about the other thing. I felt bad about it right from the start, and I kept trying to tell you, really I did, but I—just couldn't."

Lizzie didn't say anything.

Ethan plunged on desperately. "And, Lizzie, I really do like you. I—I'm glad you're my Peer Partner in math." Ethan couldn't believe he was saying this.

Lizzie's face finally melted into a smile, though there was a mischievous sparkle in her blue eyes. Ethan had never noticed how blue they were and how they lit up her whole small, freckled face.

"It's all right," she said. "I still like you. I still like you a *lot*."

Ethan never would have guessed that he would be relieved to find out that Lizzie Archer still liked him a *lot*. But right now he was, however many more poems she was going to write about him in her notebook.

At the close of eighth period, everyone returned to homeroom to get report cards. Ethan glanced quickly at his to see if there was anything on it that he needed to worry about showing his parents. Then he looked at it again. For the first time in his life, he had gotten three A's: one in science, one in math, and one in English. His work in English hadn't been that great: Ms. Leeds must have been trying to apologize to him for her accusation. But he had definitely done good work in science and math, thanks to Grace Gunderson—and to Lizzie.

Ethan hadn't planned on riding by Ms. Gunderson's apartment on his way home from school. But after he had ridden through the park, and past his old elementary school, and past the public library, his bike seemed to find its own way to the Meadows apartment complex on Alfalfa Lane. Ethan checked: The silver Honda wasn't there. He parked his bike and looked around for a place where he could watch the entrance to Apartment H16 without being seen. There was a playground on the far side of the apartment lot. He could hang out there for a while and duck behind the climbing equipment if he saw her coming.

At the playground there was only one other kid, another big kid, sitting alone on one of the swings. The kid looked up as Ethan approached him. It was Julius.

To Ethan's relief, Julius grinned at him shamefacedly. "You, too?"

Ethan returned the grin and sat down on the swing next to him. "Uh-huh," he admitted.

"Her last day," Julius said, his voice appropriately funereal.

"I know."

For the next few moments, neither one spoke. Then Julius said, "I get it now. It was all because of Grace—the science fair project, and the book report, and the tie, and everything."

"Sort of," Ethan said. Even as he said it, he knew it was only partly true. At first he had wanted to win the science fair for Grace Gunderson, but in the end he had wanted to win it for himself. "I didn't win, though."

"You should have. I thought for sure you were going to."

"But I didn't." Ethan hesitated. "So can I still be vice president of Losers, Inc.?"

Julius looked down at the ground. "Nah," he said. "You're not a real, true, genuine loser. Not anymore."

"You know what?" Ethan said. "Neither are you."

"My science fair project stank."

"You wanted it to stink."

For some reason, Ethan was reminded right then of Edison Blue. Edison had made it sound as if it were someone else's fault that he never went outside to play, but the only person who had ever stopped Edison from playing was Edison himself. *Some are born losers. Some achieve losing.* That had been Julius—and it had been Ethan, too.

He and Julius weren't losers. Neither was Lizzie. Ethan had a sudden thought. "You know who the real losers are? Alex and Marcia. They're not even sorry about what we did to Lizzie. I am, and David is, too. But they're not."

"Did Lizzie find out about the contest yet?"

"I told her."

"You did?"

"Uh-huh. It's like—I had to. I should've done it sooner. You were right, I was a creep, even though I tried to pretend I wasn't."

Julius looked relieved. "I knew you'd tell her. I didn't think you were the type to keep on going along with something mean."

The two friends grinned at each other, then both sat scuffing their feet in the icy gravel beneath the swings.

"Ethan. Julius."

At the sound of his name, spoken in that voice,

Ethan looked up. Grace Gunderson was walking toward them across the playground. The wind blew her hair around her like a golden cloak.

It was too preposterous for them to have just happened to show up *twice* at her doorstep. This time they could hardly pretend they had been riding by.

"We came to—we wanted to say goodbye," Ethan said. "We didn't really get to say goodbye in class today. We just wanted to say—we're going to miss you."

"Oh, Ethan, I'm going to miss you, too. And you, Julius. Both of you."

It wasn't exactly the right answer, but hearing it made Ethan feel better, anyway. Ms. Gunderson settled herself into the third swing, the one next to Ethan.

There was still something Ethan had to tell her. He wished he didn't have to do it in front of Julius, but he didn't know if there would ever be another moment like this.

"About Lizzie?" he began.

Ms. Gunderson gently shook her head. "You don't have to tell me anything, Ethan."

"Yes I do." He couldn't bear that she would leave not knowing the truth about him, liking him for something he wasn't. He gave Julius an anguished look. Julius mumbled something and stood up and walked over to the other edge of the playground. He sat down on one of the seesaws.

"The poem on Lizzie's science fair project? The one

that won a prize in a contest? It didn't really. Well, it did really, but not that contest, a different contest. The first contest was all a fake. Alex and Marcia set it up, and I went along because they were all making this big thing about how Lizzie liked me. And so this morning, when she was crying, it was because—they were all going to tell her, so I did."

At first Ms. Gunderson didn't say anything. Then she said, in a voice so low that Ethan had to strain to hear it, "That wasn't an easy thing for you to do, to try to right a wrong you'd committed. It sounds to me like a pretty brave thing to do. It was pretty brave of you to tell me now."

Ms. Gunderson put her finger to her lips, to silence Ethan's protest.

"And, Ethan, I want you to know that I was hoping, really hoping, that your project would be selected for the regional science fair. Were you very disappointed?"

"Not really," Ethan lied.

"I just want you to know, for what it's worth, that I think you are a remarkable young man."

"But I'm *not*." The words burst out of Ethan. "My brother's the one who's remarkable, not me. Peter Winfield. He was one of the three eighth graders who won the science fair this year. He wins every year. He's the one who's really remarkable, not me."

"I don't know your brother," Ms. Gunderson said.

She was looking so intently at Ethan that he had to drop his eyes. "I only know you. Whatever he is—and I'm sure he's remarkable, too, if you say he is—it doesn't change the truth about what *you* are."

Ethan made himself look at her. She was holding her windblown hair back from her face with one hand. He would remember her that way for the rest of his life.

Across the parking lot, Julius still sat waiting. Ethan saw him balanced awkwardly on the small seesaw, his long legs sticking out at an impossible angle. Watching him, Ethan felt a pang of loyalty and love for his former-loser friend.

He took a deep breath. There was one more thing he needed to say. "When the rest of us were mean to Lizzie? Julius was the only one who wasn't."

Ms. Gunderson smiled at him again. "Julius is a great kid," she agreed. She waved to Julius across the playground, and he rejoined them. Then she got up from the swing.

"Both of you, stop by sometime and tell me how you're doing, all right? Promise?" For a moment, Ethan thought she was going to kiss them—a teacherly kiss, not a loverly kiss—but she didn't. "When I get my first real teaching job, I only hope I have students as wonderful as the two of you."

She turned to go. Both boys watched her as she walked away.

"Man," Julius said, "what I'd give to be ten years older."

"And a foot taller," Ethan said.

At home, for the first time in weeks, Ethan measured himself. Four feet eleven! He had grown a whole half inch! But that wasn't all. He had gotten three A's on his report card. He had done a great science project, even if it hadn't won the science fair. He had read all 422 pages of *A Tale of Two Cities*. He had lost his best friend and gotten him back again. He had loved. He had been loved.

He had been trying all year to prove to the world that life was unfair. But right now life didn't seem unfair. It seemed pretty wonderful.

He heard Peter at the front door.

"Hey," he said as Peter came into the kitchen.

"Hey," Peter said.

"There's a message on the board. Mom's going to be late. Parent-teacher conferences. Mr. and Mrs. Blue."

"Should we fix something for dinner?"

"Sure," Ethan said. "How about we try another cake?"

Peter shook his head admiringly. "You don't give up, do you?"

"Nope," Ethan said. He started flipping through a cookbook. "This time let's make one that's edible.

Like—here's one that sounds good—double-chocolate fudge cake."

Peter draped his jacket over the back of a kitchen chair. Ethan tied on his dad's big apron.

"Move over, Betty Crocker," Ethan said. "Here we come!"

CLAUDIA MILLS is the author of many books for children, including *Dinah Forever* (Hyperion Paperbacks for Children). She teaches philosophy at the University of Colorado, in Boulder, where she lives with her husband and their two sons.